A Parliament of Crows

Alan M. Clark

IFD Publishing
P.O. Box 40776, Eugene, Oregon 97404 U.S.A.
www.ifdpublishing.com

Originally published by Lazy Fascist Press.

Acknowledgments

Thanks to Cameron Pierce, Eric Witchey, Jill Bauman, Elizabeth Engstrom, Pigg, Mole, Lorelei Shannon, Marti McKenna, Vernon T. Williams, Laurie Ewing McNichols, Molly Tanzer, Mark Roland, Linda Addison, Frank Freemon, Susan Stockell, Kirsten Alene, and Melody Kees Clark.

Author's Note

A Parliament of Crows is a historical fiction novel inspired by the criminal activities of the three infamous Wardlaw sisters. In writing the story, I've changed their names and some of the place names. For purposes of storytelling, I have not adhered strictly to their history and where needed I created scenarios out of whole cloth to further the plot.

The lives of the Wardlaw sisters began before the American Civil War and ended early in the twentieth century. They had a habit of wearing mourning clothes and living in dwellings with few furnishings. Accomplished educators, they took positions of prominence within communities, but were secretive and wary of those outside the family, and would drop their responsibilities and flee suddenly if they anticipated the slightest threat. Several close members of their family turned up dead under extraordinary circumstances. Eventually, they generated enough suspicion that they were arrested and charged with murder.

Because the information about the Wardlaw sisters gives a rather two dimensional view of them, I can't help but wonder about their emotional characteristics. I'm curious about the choices they made that led to their crimes, and how they justified to themselves what they did even as they went about their dreadful business. *A Parliament of Crows* is my exploration of the possibilities with the use of fictional characters and the fun of storytelling.

—Alan M. Clark
Eugene, Oregon

A Parliament of Crows

Alan M. Clark

Publishing
Eugene, Oregon

The shame of Vertiline's incarceration had abated little in the eighteen months since her arrest. Believing herself nearly helpless against the forces controlling her fate, she expressed the slight power that remained to her in a simple reminder spoken aloud each morning while sitting on the bunk in her jail cell: "After what they did during the war, they have no right to judge us. Maintain a sense of personal dignity, for you are useless to your sisters without it."

The state of New Jersey had indicted jointly Miss Vertiline Mortlow, sixty-one years of age, and her fifty-nine-year-old twin sisters, Mrs. Mary Mortlow Sneed, and Mrs. Carolee Mortlow Marshall. They were charged with insurance fraud and the murder of Carolee's daughter, Orphia Marshall Sneed. The young woman had been found dead in the bathtub of the sisters' East Orange apartment, lying in a few inches of cold water, her head below the faucet, and her feet hanging over the back of the tub. Although suspicious, her death was at first seen as suicide. When Vertiline and her sisters tried to collect on several insurance policies they had taken out on Orphia, the police began an investigation and the sisters were arrested.

In the long delay before the trial, during which the sisters were kept in separate jail cells, the twins had perhaps suffered the most. Based on what her attorney said of his visits with them, Vertiline feared that Mary intentionally starved herself and that Carolee had gone mad from the isolation.

As the time drew near for the sisters to appear in court, Vertiline felt an unaccountable excitement despite her dread. After endless days of boredom spent in her lonely cell, she anticipated that the trial would provide intellectual and emotional stimulation. She hated herself for looking forward to the event.

On the first day of trial—the first time she'd seen the twins in over a month—while riding in the police van to the courthouse, Vertiline tried to make eye contact with her sisters. Carolee's eyes darted about warily. When spoken to, she appeared startled, even frightened at times. Mary, her eyes downcast, was emaciated and uncommunicative. She flinched and cringed whenever Carolee became agitated.

"Are you well?" Vertiline asked them several times in different ways and with increasing urgency. Their answers held little information.

As the trial commenced in the courtroom with the prosecution presenting its case, Vertiline struggled to put her fears aside and look for ways to aid in her own defense. Torn between the urgency of concern for her sisters, and the need to maintain awareness of the proceedings, her head ached, her heart beat uncomfortably in her chest, and she struggled to take deep breaths.

In defense of her own sanity, her mind turned briefly to pleasant recollection.

Vertiline had spent a childhood of privilege in a home on Spring Street in Milledgeville, Georgia. Having recalled innumerable times the magical summer parties her mother, Abigale Sobearn Mortlow, hosted in the garden behind the house, Vertiline easily found vivid memories of the events within her mind. She could *see* the beautiful guests, their eyes cheerful, movements graceful and gracious, their clothing exquisite. She *heard* their happy voices, full of charm and wit. The exotic decorations and extravagant tables of food and drink were there, filled with dishes prepared from Ducy's delicious recipes by the cook. Vertiline could almost taste the buttered spoonbread, the fried fish, and chess pie. As dusk approached amidst the gentle murmur of the guests, Abigale move about, a silent white bell in her crinoline, lighting colorful Chinese paper lanterns strung on cane poles. Lightning bugs rose from the warm earth of the flower beds, their soft greenish yellow glow competing with the warm flickering orange flames within the lanterns.

Bitter-sweet, the magic light inevitably faded from the garden with the memory of losing Abigale to pneumonia brought on by influenza. Vertiline had been seven years old when her mother died. For all the crisp memories of the garden parties, her recollections of Abigale had wilted, her lovely features having faded from memory.

Thankfully, the warmth and love of her father, Georgia Supreme Court Justice Horace G. Mortlow, always remained in full bloom. Though he had long ago passed away, her memories of him were clear. He was truly the only authority to whom she must answer. Surely, he would understand what she and her sisters had done and why, and would not judge them too harshly.

Her breath more even, her heart calmed somewhat, Vertiline's awareness returned to the courtroom.

The judge, a tall, lean man with a bushy brow named Tolland, spoke from the bench to Mary, "Mrs. Sneed, please sit upright and show the court due respect."

Vertiline wanted to say that her sister wasn't a child to be reprimanded for her behavior, but held her tongue.

Within moments, Mary had slumped forward in her chair again. Judge Tolland seemed to notice, but said nothing until her head fell forward, lolling upon the table.

Then discussions began concerning the poor condition of Mrs. Mary Mortlow Sneed, and Judge Tolland adjourned the trial for the day.

To stave off despair, Vertiline tried to believe in what her father had always called "the hope of tomorrow."

Chapter 2
Mary—Sacrifice

Confined to a jail cell, Mary experienced boredom, but not loneliness. Whether she liked it or not, her twin sister, Carolee, was always with her, even if not in a physical sense. Her connection to her twin's thoughts, feelings, and memories, had real advantages, but disadvantages existed as well. While the two understood each other with an uncommonly thorough knowing, conflict and resentment existed between them much as it did with most sisters.

Mary didn't want to eat the shiny brown cockroach that had wandered into her jail cell, but Carolee was insistent, and she was used to getting her way. The campaign to make the disgusting insects seem more palatable had begun when Carolee found out that Mary had stopped eating. The bland food in the jail wasn't enough to maintain good health, and Mary knew that her twin ate every insect she could get her hands on. Carolee was an animal, her concerns those of an animal. Her experiences during The War Between the States had left her that way, but until recently she'd been good at keeping up appearances.

Repeatedly, Carolee shared with Mary her memories of eating the roaches: The texture, the flavor, the tiny surge of energy gained from the sustenance, and the crumbs of satisfaction she derived from it. Because the two sisters occupied separate cells in different wings of the building, though, Carolee could urge all she wanted, but she couldn't make Mary eat it.

As the insect scurried out of the cell and disappeared down the corridor, Mary put it out of her mind. A moment later, Carolee's insistence ceased, and Mary relaxed.

With the way she was presently treated by her sister, the idea of loneliness had become intriguing. Mary had never truly understood how others felt when they said they were lonesome. At the moment she would willingly experience the feeling and the release it would offer from her sister's badgering.

That was a fantasy, though. Real relief would come soon. If she continued her fast, she would not have to wait long for her reward in heaven.

The cockroach, or perhaps a new one, returned and poked about in the corner of the cell. Mary tried not to think about it, but most of all she tried not to be disgusted by the creature so Carolee might not become aware of it.

Because communication through their invisible connection did not allow for words, deception was rare and difficult, although Mary had found that if she suppressed her feelings about a certain matter, she could keep the knowledge and experience of it from her sister for a short time.

Mary couldn't help being repelled by the movements of the roach's twig-like legs. Carolee's urgings resumed—Mary shouldn't have watched it.

But, no, She wouldn't eat the insect and she wouldn't eat the food the jail provided either. A guard removed from her cell the rough crockery bowl containing her meals after thirty minutes, whether she touched the food or not. She gestured toward a set of shelves on the opposite side of the passage from her cell. "It's over there," she told the cockroach, hoping it might leave the cell so she could stop thinking about it, and Carolee would leave her alone. "Go eat," she said, a disturbing tremor in her voice.

Not one of God's favored, the insect had no ability to understand—the creature ignored her.

Carolee kept up the pressure on Mary to eat it.

Past the painful stage of starvation, Mary felt a light euphoria. When she closed her eyes, beautiful blue and orange shapes swam in her field of vision. She knew the condition represented a weakening of her system that would lead to death. Her father had made the same sacrifice when food supplies were low during the War to ensure his children's survival. Mary saw it as right and proper that she should do the same for her sisters. If only her twin would make the sacrifice, it would go a long way toward thwarting the state of New Jersey's case against Vertiline. Carolee had always been selfish, though. She feared she'd cease to exist. She didn't seem to understand that being a Mortlow meant something in the eyes of the Lord.

Carolee increased her efforts, trying to prevent Mary from thinking of anything but the act of eating roaches.

The increasing euphoria from lack of sustenance helped Mary ignore her sister. She lay on the chill, damp floor of her cell, watching the insect, trying to relax, and let go of her flesh. With time, her thoughts became more independent.

Mary recalled that when she was young, her father referred to her as "the quiet one." What he couldn't know was that whenever Mary needed to express frustration, throw a temper tantrum or break something in anger, Carolee did it for her. In return, Mary always provided thoughtful calm and quiet reasoning for her sister.

Carolee led the way for both of them because of her aggressive nature, but that didn't mean she wouldn't consider Mary's point of view. Shortly after they turned twelve years old, Carolee dared her twin to push a slave down the stairs. While willing to participate in such mischief as a witness and coconspirator, Mary didn't want to personally commit the crime. If she had not done it, however, Carolee would have kept at her, becoming a relentless irritation.

The twins hid in the guest room that opened to the left off the top of the stairs. Although the door was opened a crack, the drawn shades within the room provided plenty of concealing shadow. They listened and watched through the crack in the door for their prey. Carolee most often perpetrated the misdeeds, but Mary liked the activity and vicariously experiencing her sister's emotions. Most of all, she enjoyed the stalking of their prey. Restless Carolee fidgeted while she waited, but the process taught Mary patience and how to keep herself entertained by pondering possibilities.

Who would suffer today? One of the young female slaves? If it turned out to be a strong adult male like Jasper, might he get up and retaliate? The question brought with it trepidation, but Mary reassured herself that such action taken by a slave was extremely unlikely.

Lost in thought, she didn't hear the footsteps on the landing.

"Now!" Carolee said, shoving Mary out the door. Mary blundered into the slave, Agnes, who had an armload of table linens. Agnes, wide-eyed and open-mouthed, turned as she stumbled, and bounced off the banister newel. She threw out her grasping hands for something to stop her fall. A table cloth blossomed out and fell; napkins flew up like fluttering white doves. The sound of the fall was interminable, an alarm that would surely bring consequences. Agnes made a rough backwards somersault down the stairs, hit the floor with a loud smack, and lay there gasping and moaning.

The twins remained at the top of the stairs while Mr. Mortlow and his servant Merrill entered the hall below to investigate. Vertiline emerged from her upstairs bedroom. Eyeing the twins critically, she moved past them and joined the men below.

Agnes's forearm had taken on an alarming shape, a bone within crooked and straining to emerge from stretched skin. Mary knew her twin relished the intense emotions of the moment. Carolee was about to draw everyone's attention and claim responsibility.

Mary wouldn't stand for that. To assert her own desires instead, she jabbed her twin with an elbow.

Carolee backed down silently and removed the smile from her rosy cheeks, and just in time too, for everyone gathered around Agnes in the hall below looked up at the twins in horror.

Although Mary felt no pride in what they had done, she also felt no shame, and would never betray her twin with a confession. She donned her most innocent look.

Even so, if not for Vertiline, they would have been severely punished that day.

Chapter 3
Carolee—Survival

Pacing the characterless six by eight cell, Carolee nearly kicked over the slop bucket beside the bed. She'd become so absorbed in her connection with her sister, and so upset with her, she'd briefly lost all awareness of her surroundings. She sat on the thin mattress and pushed the bucket closer to the wall with her foot.

Carolee knew what Mary was up to and didn't like it. Although Mary had tried to conceal the truth, Carolee had slowly become aware that her sister was suffering and losing weight. Indeed, the more lightheaded and weak Mary got, the easier it became for Carolee to access her twin's thoughts and feelings.

Mary intended to honor their father's sacrifice with her own. For Carolee, honor was a costume that only the wealthy could afford, one that didn't wear well with time. She was certain Mary had no recollection of Mr. Mortlow's true sacrifice, his real gift to his daughters. Carolee recalled vividly, but she would not relate the memory to her sister.

That Mary was willing to throw away her life disgusted Carolee. Mary believed in things Carolee gave up as nonsense long ago—Mary believed in God and Jesus, and that she and her sisters were somehow better than other people. The war taught Carolee that despite outward appearance, there was no difference between aristocrats and the common people, between gentlefolk and persons considered coarse or uncouth. She was raised in privilege, given a good education, and had cultivated good manners and refined tastes. But when the War forced her to endure privation, in order to survive she'd readily done what, by the standards of her upbringing, was unthinkable.

Carolee was a survivor. When she thought about what that meant, she often remembered the emaciated feral dog that prepared a whelping den and gave birth to a litter of pups under an azalea in the garden behind the house on Spring Street. Because the war had finally come to Milledgeville and Union forces moved through the city, Mr. Mortlow had instructed his daughters to confine themselves to the upstairs of the house. They were not allowed to go outside at all. Carolee snuck out to the garden anyway, and was attracted by the small squeals of the pups. The bitch and her suckling litter was such a sweet vision, Carolee had an impulse to pick up and cuddle one of the cute puppies. A glaring look and snarls from the mother persuaded her to keep her distance. Carolee did not begrudge the bitch such brute protection of her young. She dragged a couple of the wrought-iron outdoor chairs over to the exposed side of the azalea to help block the cold November wind from the den. Having something warm and tender to think about, Carolee returned to the house without being caught. For the first time in a long while, she looked forward to the next day when she would find another opportunity to sneak out and look in on the nursery.

When the next day came, Vertiline kept a close watch on her, insisting that she play games with her twin and help with various small tasks while remaining in either their father's upstairs study or the hiding place accessible through the wall panel in that room. Mr. Mortlow created the secret room months before in preparation for a time when the family might need to hide from marauding Union troops. The family currently slept there every night. Carolee was sick of the cramped, smelly space.

Mr. Mortlow had been asleep in his chair at his desk in the study all day. He was white as bedlinen and sleeping soundly. The four of them took naps in the afternoon. Mr. Mortlow often slept in his chair while his daughters lay on piles of quilts in the hiding place. When nap time came, Carolee said, "I'm going to take a quilt into the study and sleep with Father today."

Vertiline didn't argue with that, but because she left the panel to the hiding place open, Carolee would have to make sure everyone was asleep before she snuck out to see the puppies. She made a little bed beside her father's desk near the opening, just out of her sisters' line of sight. When she heard them breathing deeply in sleep, she got up and snuck out of the study, tiptoed down the stairs, through the hall, the dining room, the kitchen, and out the back door.

She crept through the garden, approaching the whelping den quietly to keep from startling the bitch and her litter. As she slowly pulled one of the chairs away, she heard growling. Light spilled into the den, revealing the bitch licking her bloody mouth. The litter was gone, all but for one tiny leg. The bitch lunged and Carolee gasped, dropped the chair, and stumbled back. Heartbroken, she turned and ran for the house.

All day, Carolee struggled to hide her tears.

Finally, Vertiline asked her, "Why are you so sad today?"

"I wish the War was over," Carolee said, "and we could all have plenty to eat again." That opened her up and she was overwhelmed with emotion. She cried like a baby while Vertiline held her.

Carolee was angry with the bitch for eating her pups, but had sympathy for the animal as well—she too was hungry.

Before the end of the war, Carolee was forced by necessity to eat something much worse. When she did, she relished it, knowing that with the nourishment she would live a little longer. Indeed, that was all she wanted—to live. Beyond wishful thinking, there was no reason to believe in an afterlife.

She knew Mary was willing to sacrifice her life to save her family, but Carolee wasn't going to lose her sister, half of herself, to such a useless gesture.

Reaching again to access her sister's experience, she became aware that Mary was disturbed by the appearance of another cockroach. Carolee pressed her eyes shut tight and concentrated on persuading her twin to eat the insect. She hoped the nourishment might stimulate Mary's hunger so she would more willingly eat the food the jail provided. With insistence and attention to detail, she repeatedly imagined what she herself had done countless times in her cell, the process of catching the insects and stuffing them in her mouth. She recalled as vividly as possible the texture of the chiton and the meager fatty flesh, slightly salty, as it moved across her tongue and down her throat. She relived the experience over and over, communicating every aspect of her satisfaction with the insect consumption.

Chapter 4
Vertiline—Carnival Atmosphere

Tuesday morning, a deputy at the jail informed Vertiline that Mary was too ill to appear in court.

Mary needs her rest, Vertiline told herself, trying unsuccessfully to set aside worries about her sister.

As she and Carolee rode to the courthouse, a slovenly rabble ran along beside the police van, shouting obscenities and shaking fists. Vertiline kept her head down to avoid seeing the spittle that flew against the small windows.

The shuddering movements of the vehicle tormented her arthritic joints. She hated the rattling contraption, much as she hated the rabble, in an unreasoning manner both satisfying and discomfiting. She knew that most people thought of automobiles as a shining example of ingenuity, as an indication that man's future was bright.

If I'm convicted, perhaps I will not have to suffer that future.

Something, a bottle perhaps, broke against the side of the van and Vertiline's heart leapt into her throat.

"They're restless," Carolee said. "These people are already tired of waiting." Her blue eyes were wide with fear beneath her dark veil.

Vertiline raised one eyebrow, her silent questioning look.

"For our hanging," Carolee answered flatly.

"You know there are worse things than being hanged," Vertiline said.

Carolee nodded vaguely, the lines in her pale, aging face deep and fretful.

Just before the van turned down an alley to reach the entrance at the back of the courthouse, Vertiline saw through the saliva-streaked windows that the crowd out front of the stately building had grown twice as large as it had been the day before.

As the trial progressed through the day, Carolee's agitation in the courtroom became pronounced, her eyes darting about, her head frequently cocked to one side, her facial expressions changing as if in response to communication from an imaginary person. Again, Vertiline could not concentrate on the proceedings as she devoted her attention to helping her sister remain calm—sitting close, holding Carolee's hand, and providing an occasional reassuring smile. In the end, the madness won out. Carolee interrupted the proceedings while the prosecutor (Polackski or something with more syllables) questioned Dr. Robert Casby, the one who had provided the sisters with the certificate of health required to take out the life insurance policies on Orphia.

"*You* killed her!" Carolee shouted at the doctor, the volume and emotion in her voice silencing the courtroom. "Help me, Mary, or all is lost!" Carolee then began beating her head against the defense table. Of course, Mary wasn't in the courtroom. Judge Tolland demanded Carolee's removal. Two bailiffs had little trouble subduing her. Vertiline was disturbed to see Carolee's flailing arms and rigid legs. The bailiffs removed her, and Vertiline would later learn that Carolee was taken to a sanatorium and put under observation.

Wednesday arrived with an overcast morning, and Vertiline rode in the van without her sisters, feeling none too fit herself after the barrel-chested guard who'd helped her into the van spoke to her. "I always know which prisoners are guilty," he said. The chill of his hands, evident through Vertiline's sleeve as he provided a steadying grip at her elbow, matched that of his words. "I can see it in their eyes. You wear the veil and try to look away, but I can still see it. I *know*." Then he smiled.

He will never know, none of them will ever know what was in our hearts, Vertiline reassured herself.

Again, an angry rabble, shouting and cursing, followed the van. The vehicle paused before turning down the alley that led to the back of the courthouse. Vertiline heard the driver yell, "Get that wagon out of the way," but she couldn't see to whom he spoke. The guards who rode with him in the front of the van stepped out and worked to clear the boisterous rabble from the intersection, lunging with their truncheons and shouting, "Move along!" The mob shouted insults at the guards, then ran off down the block.

Despite the increased frailty she'd experienced in recent years, Vertiline did not suffer from poor eyesight. She looked through a window relatively free of spittle and saw the rabble merge with the throng on the courthouse steps half a block away. The crowd, consisting primarily of laborers, had grown since the day before. Many children, truant from school or perhaps released from their lessons to join the cruel celebration, moved among the adults. Vertiline could see vendors of food and other items, perhaps the souvenirs and tabloids full of lies her attorney had told her about. Performers, including a troupe of red-and-green-clad acrobats, kept the crowd entertained. The carnival atmosphere belied the solemnity of the court itself.

Vertiline saw the trial as an absurd pretense, a plot to destroy her and her sisters, not for what they'd done, but because they represented the culture of the South. Worse, no doubt the State found the trial a boon because it brought needed attention and commerce to the city of Newark. From the sensational newspaper headlines her attorney had shown her, it

21

was clear that the press and the state worked together toward her conviction, for the people of New Jersey and New York had already decided the case. Indeed, the prosecution's arguments against her were predicated in part on evidence gathered by a journalist.

More than anything, Vertiline desired an escape, but she was too old to be slippery, to escape bodily from her predicament. The guards in her escort from jail to court and back again each day were not vigilant, but sufficient for an old woman with arthritis in her feet, knees, hips, shoulders, and elbows. And, of course, she had her sisters to consider as well.

After arriving at the courthouse, guards took her through the Tombs, a place of sharp echoes in the basement of the building with meeting rooms and lonely holding cells. She'd sat in one of the pale green meeting rooms the previous day, waiting with her attorney for court to begin, and assumed she would presently suffer more of the same, but instead the guards guided her up the dank staircase into the courtroom and placed her in a seat at the defense table next to her attorney.

He didn't acknowledged her presence in any way as he sat reading from loose leaves of paper. An untidy, plump man who went by the name of Hitchens, he was in so many ways an unfinished fellow. He always smelled of rancid fat.

Feeling very much alone, Vertiline watched everyone file into the courtroom. The prosecutor entered and approached the prosecution table. She had hated the sickly little man the first time she met him several months ago, and she hated him still. He was olive-skinned, and his short, thin frame made his clothing look too big. His northern surname—an immigrant name of Eastern European origin—wasn't memorable because of its difficult pronunciation.

The prosecutor stood not ten feet away, but didn't look in Vertiline's direction. Kalinowski—that was it, an ugly Polish name. Thankfully, his discourteous behavior allowed her to ignore him in return.

The grand scale of the chamber, the fine quality of its woodwork, and the graceful curve of the wall behind the judge's bench gave the courtroom a solemn, imposing air. How could such an atmosphere of authority continue to exist under such corrupt circumstances? Surely the courthouse must crumble and fall any moment, the illusion dashed.

Finally Mr. Hitchens turned to Vertiline. "Good morning, Miss Mortlow." He gave her no time to respond to his greeting. "Because Mrs. Marshall is under observation at the sanatorium, and Mrs. Sneed is too ill to join us in court," he said, "the judge has granted a severance of your cases. Your sisters' trials will be postponed for now, but yours will continue."

Again, the responsibility for her family rested entirely on Vertiline's shoulders. She knew that if her sisters survived to be tried, the outcome of her trial would be a determining factor in theirs. She sagged beneath the weight of the responsibility for a moment, but then thought better of it and sat up straight again, the fabric of her black silk clothing rustling, her chair squeaking.

During the morning's proceedings, Mr. Kalinowski questioned a handwriting expert, a Mr. Beaumont, about several different suicide notes stored in Vertiline's correspondence folio. The folio had been found by a journalist who illegally searched the sisters' basement apartment after the police completed their inspection of the premises. He then turned the folio over to the prosecution.

Watching the so-called expert, Vertiline thought he appeared to be slightly inebriated. "The handwriting in the suicide notes is identical to the handwriting examples belonging to Miss Vertiline Mortlow," he said.

Did he have to salve his conscience with drink before he could testify against me?

On cross-examination, Mr. Hitchens asked, "Could the handwriting of a student be identical to that of his teacher?"

"I cannot say without seeing the document compared to an exemplar," Mr. Beaumont said.

Mr. Hitchens remained mute during the prosecution's questioning of the lead investigator on the case, Detective Robert Walker. Despite his name, Vertiline thought the dark-haired man looked Greek or perhaps Italian.

"Please tell us what Mrs. Carolee Mortlow Marshall told you concerning the death of the young Mrs. Orphia Marshall Sneed," Mr. Kalinowski said to the witness.

"She told me the young woman had drowned," he said flatly.

"Did the evidence support that, Detective Walker?" Mr. Kalinowski raised his eyebrows to signal his own doubt.

"I cannot say," Detective Walker responded. "The bathtub in which she was found contained only three inches of water."

Mr. Kalinowski held out his right hand toward the twelve men of the jury and spread his delicate thumb and forefinger apart three inches. "Does this look something like the depth to which you refer?" he asked, the corners of his mouth turned down. His expression was obviously meant to convey his skepticism that anyone might drown on their own in so little water.

Despite her distracted state on the first day of the trail, Vertiline had heard the coroner testify that he had found Orphia severely malnour-

23

ished and that there was evidence she'd been addicted to narcotics. He'd given the cause of her death as drowning and said that apparently she had ingested a large dose of laudanum prior to the event.

Mr. Hitchens in cross-examination had asked if the drowning might have occurred because Orphia lost consciousness in her intoxicated state while lying in the bathtub and her head slipped beneath the surface of the water. The coroner had agreed that was possible.

At present, Vertiline did not miss the fact that in his questioning of Detective Walker, Mr. Kalinowski wanted to give the jury the idea that Orphia was forcibly drowned.

"Did Miss Vertiline Mortlow tell you what she believed had motivated her niece to commit suicide?" Mr. Kalinowski asked.

"She said Mrs. Orphia Sneed was depressed over the loss of her husband and having to give her daughter up for adoption," Detective Walker said.

Again, the look of skepticism on the face of the prosecutor. The judge made no effort to reprimand Mr. Kalinowski, and Mr. Hitchens did not challenge him either. Frustrated, Vertiline looked down at the tabletop to avoid watching Mr. Kalinowski's continued theatrics.

"She spoke of the loss of only one child?" Mr. Kalinowski said.

"That's correct," Detective Walker said.

Further questioning revealed that Orphia had a second child, an infant that had gone missing just prior to the family moving from Brooklyn to East Orange, New Jersey, and that none within the family had notified the local authorities in New York of the disappearance.

"I still don't think this is relevant," Vertiline whispered to Mr. Hitchens. "Challenge him!"

He waved her demand away.

Vertiline fumed as Detective Walker's testimony continued. The most incriminating revelation he had to offer was that the sisters held three insurance policies for Orphia, totaling thirty-two thousand dollars.

"I have no further questions, Your Honor," Mr. Kalinowski said.

"Does council wish to cross examine the witness?" the judge asked.

"No, Your Honor," Mr. Hitchens said.

He is worthless! Vertiline wanted to strike her attorney in the face.

"The witness is excused," the judge said.

"The prosecution rests, Your Honor," Mr. Kalinowski said.

During the break for lunch, Vertiline and Mr. Hitchens sat at a table in one of the green meeting rooms in the Tombs. "You should have made more effort to challenge the prosecution," she said, disgusted.

"I know the law," he said impatiently, looking away. "If I had challenged the relevance of the missing infant, the prosecutor would have pointed out that your family's efforts to obstruct justice in the case of the infant shows a pattern of conspiracy. Conspiracy is at the heart of the prosecutions theory that you and your sisters murdered your niece to gain the insurance payout."

Vertiline glared at Mr. Hitchens.

"We'd have a better chance if you would take the witness stand," he said. "If you testify, you'll be able to respond to much of the circumstantial evidence the state is using to characterize you and your sisters as criminals."

Vertiline had been adamant against testifying in her own defense whenever Mr. Hitchens brought the subject up. Avoiding the scrutiny of others had always been important. Her present predicament, had made that all but impossible. If she allowed her attorney to question her, the prosecution would have the right to cross-examine.

Mr. Hitchens rubbed his pudgy, pink-speckled nose. "Their case against you is based purely on circumstantial evidence and rumor. That's clear to everyone. If the jury hears you speak, they'll know you for the refined educator you are and won't hand down a conviction."

"They don't like me," she said. "I'm a private person who doesn't take to others readily. There's no guarantee they will like me any better to hear me speak."

Mr. Hitchens looked at her squarely, and remained silent.

Vertiline wanted to say no to him again, but she was more receptive to his suggestion than she would have anticipated. Her attorney wasn't doing much good on his own, and she might find ways to improve her chances of acquittal while answering his questions. The twelve members of the jury looked like the sort of men she might easily cajole to her point of view, even if they didn't like her. But Mr. Hitchens's direct examination of her would not be the end of her testimony.

"The judge holds the prosecution to no standards of procedure or decorum," she said. "If I take the stand, the prosecutor will want to cross-examine, and when he does, he'll cause no end of trouble. If you don't object, the judge will allow—"

"I must choose my battles carefully," Mr. Hitchens said. "If anything, the prosecution's questions are poorly phrased. If I object, he'll merely re-phrase what he's said and the jury will hear it twice, giving it emphasis."

A convenient lawyerly response. Still, Mr. Hitchens's argument rang true; the jury would be more sympathetic to Vertiline after hearing her speak.

The prospect of cross-examination by the weaselly prosecutor was daunting, but she'd weather that storm when the time arrived.

"Promise me you'll make more of an effort to challenge that little man," Vertiline said.

"I will look for every reasonable opportunity," he said evenly.

"Very well," she said, the words a bitter persimmon on her tongue. "I'll take the witness stand."

"I can see you are distraught about it," he said. "I'll have several witnesses before you, but I will try not to make you wait too long."

When she was a child, people presumed and looked for only the best from Vertiline, especially her father, and because she wanted to live up to expectations, she tried to be a good girl. That time and place seemed long ago and far away.

Chapter 5
Vertiline—Childhood

After Abigale died, Vertiline's father made special efforts to fill his wife's shoes. Although duties required him to travel much of the time, when home he spent time with his daughters in the parlor in the evenings. He read aloud to Vertiline and the twins before bedtime from picture books and adventure stories, the sound of his warm, deep voice a comfort even when the stories became frightening. Each of the girls vied for the special privilege of sitting in his lap to better see the illustrations. He played games with them and took them on picnics. He told them stories about his young life.

Vertiline's favorite was the one about a duel he'd had with a prideful man named Clarence Perforce Tate. She'd heard him tell the tale at one of Abigale's garden parties. No one ever believed the account, but it was still a good yarn. When the twins reached eight years of age, he told the story to them, and Vertiline was pleased to hear it again.

"This man, Tate," he began, "was known for dueling. A rich man from Atlanta, he could take most anything he wanted. Folks said he had killed fifteen men in pistol duels over the years. He bragged about it, and looked for opportunities to increase his numbers. Rumor had it that he was so proud, he used bullets made of solid gold."

"Tell them what he said about using those bullets, Father," Vertiline said.

Mr. Mortlow thrust out his chin, looked down his long nose and said in a pompous manner, "'It's a good investment. Shoot a man with gold and he won't get back up again.'"

The twins' faces held identical wide-eyed grimaces, as Mr. Mortlow nodded slowly.

"So then he met Mother while you two were courting," Vertiline interrupted.

"Don't get ahead of me, sweetheart. Yes, he took an interest in your mother. I knew to avoid him, but he said dastardly things to her."

"What did he say, Father?" Carolee asked, her eager eyes glinting in the lamplight.

"I am too much a gentleman to repeat them." A grave expression settled on his face briefly. "Although frightened by his fierce reputation, I could not allow his words to go unchallenged."

"You loved Mother *so* much!" Mary said, her eyes wide with surprise and delight.

"Yes, I did," Mr. Mortlow said, smiling. "I confronted him. He lied, and then insulted me."

Vertiline watched the twins. They looked worried, but smiled when their father took on a comical look of surprise.

"I became so angry, I forgot my fear and challenged him to a duel!"

They laughed nervously. "No, you didn't," Carolee said with a grimace.

"Yes, I did. On a gray morning we met in an open field. We were presented with a dueling set. He loaded a solid gold ball into his pistol, saying, 'I'm going to fire this shot straight and true into your heart.'"

"Stop," Mary said. "I don't want to hear!"

"He didn't succeed, silly," Vertiline said. "You're sitting on his lap, after all."

"When the time came for us to fire, I managed to get off the first shot." Mr. Mortlow beamed. "He fell dead, and when I tried to step away, I too fell. I had taken his gold shot in my leg!"

"Ouch!" the twins said in unison.

"It's still in there," he said, laughing. "You're sitting on it right now, Mary."

She leapt off his lap, laughing. Carolee put her hands to her mouth and giggled.

"I'm saving it, you see. You can imagine it's worth quite a lot. If we ever run on hard times, I will cut it out and we'll be rich again."

"Father, how awful!" Vertiline cried, delighted. The story had gotten better with the retelling. A man of average height, his hair already graying substantially in his mid-forties and with a slight potbelly, her father might not be the brave man from his outlandish story, but he was their hero nonetheless.

"Now everyone off to bed," Mr. Mortlow said.

The giggling children ran out of the parlor and up the stairs to their room. The twins jumped in bed and soon slept.

Vertiline stayed up, against her father's wishes. Sitting at her tiny child's desk, working by candlelight, she wrote the story of her father's duel in her journal titled "My Book of Memories."

Chapter 6
Mary—Destitute

Mary's continuing efforts to let go of her flesh were frustrated as a pain in her lower left leg, a remnant of an injury Carolee had given her decades earlier, kept drawing her back to the experience of her body. Shortly after the end of the War and the death of their father in 1865, during the first year of their financial tribulation, the threat of Carolee's aggressive nature and uncontrolled emotion had given Mary and Vertiline much worry, her occasional outbursts creating calamity and bringing unwanted attention.

On one occasion, Carolee severely harmed Mary and herself. The three sisters had gone to the Currington Bank to transfer funds to pay the mortgage on their house and property. A northern company had assumed controlling interest in the bank. Except for the blue-clad federal soldiers who served as security, the bank was still staffed with men who had always been a part of the community. The sisters sat in the office of the bank manager, Mr. Bertram Wagoner, a man who habitually dressed in brown clothing and had a head shaped like a block.

"Miss Mortlow," he said to Vertiline, "your father invested heavily in Confederate bonds which now have no value."

"I have currency." She pulled a stack of one-hundred dollar Confederate notes from her bag. Mr. Mortlow had put the bills in a tin box, along with other items of value, and buried that in the garden over a year ago. They smelled of mildew, but otherwise appeared in good condition, the picture on the top bill, of slaves loading a wagon with cotton, as clear as the day the note was printed.

"The Confederacy printed so many of those as to render them worthless," Wagoner said, exasperation in his tone. "I'm sure you're well aware of the inflation and the riots of the past few years."

He doesn't want to help us, Mary thought. *What have we done?*

Vertiline, clearly troubled, rallied quickly. "Mr. Wagoner, we've done business with your bank for over ten years. Surely—"

"Miss Mortlow, I was never a secessionist," he said, leaning back and folding his arms, "and I strongly believe in the Federal reconstruction effort."

He's turned on his own people, Mary thought. Her impression of Mr. Wagoner changed in an instant. No longer was he a benevolent man of the community. In her young mind, he'd become a vile usurper of local commerce, a pirate of sorts. *He's what folks are calling a carpetbagger.* She wanted to see him harmed.

Mary felt Carolee's ire rising, and took uneasy glances in her direction.

"Your father supported secession," Mr Wagoner said, "which ultimately brought ruin upon our community. Many suffered during the war, and now many who were fortunate before the war must help pay—"

Carolee leapt from her seat. She lifted her chair and threw it at the man. It bounced off the edge of his walnut desk and struck Mary in the shin. Carolee echoed Mary's cry of pain. As she bent to clutch her shin, she saw Carolee do the same.

Mr. Wagoner screamed and tried to get to the door, most likely to call for his Yankee security.

Clever Vertiline was quicker. She opened the door and shouted, "Help us! He's harmed my sisters!"

The bank lobby held numerous customers, no doubt with troubles similar to those of the Mortlows. All eyes turned toward the sisters as they left the manager's office, Mary and her twin hanging onto Vertiline and limping, their faces darkened with pain. As the Mortlows moved toward the entrance to the bank, the customers fixed their attention on Mr. Wagoner standing in the doorway to his office.

Someone murmured, "Scalawag," but that was most likely the limit of the customers' belligerence—they couldn't afford to offend the bank manager. Still, their withering stares provided protection of a sort, since Mr. Wagoner ceased to follow the Mortlows out and didn't call for Carolee's arrest. Despite the pain and the need to find help for her swollen leg, Mary looked back and saw Mr. Wagoner shake his head, retreat back into his office, and close the door.

"Coward!" Carolee shouted as they left the building.

Vertiline hurried them to see their doctor. As they sat waiting in his all-white examination room, she whispered with downcast eyes and a pale complexion, "We are destitute."

With shame, Mary could only wonder if the aspect of poverty already cloaked them. Could people see it? "What will we do?" she asked.

"I'll think of something," Vertiline said.

Oh, Lord, help us to survive, Mary prayed, and wondered briefly if her silent plea was heard. *Of course God heard,* she told herself. *He loves our family. He will protect us and show the way.*

Mary was in a splint and starched bandages for months with a broken fibula, and although Carolee's injury could not be established medically, she too was off her feet and on crutches for much of that time. During their convalescence, the twins spent time in the Browning

Hospital in Milledgeville.

The Mortlows lost the house on Spring Street in the fall of 1865. Vertiline temporarily took up residence in the Etlinger Hotel in town while she arranged for the three of them to move to Virginia to live with their grandmother, Winifred Sobearn, who owned a small women's college. Because the hotel had suffered fire damage during the War, and parts of it were still blackened and closed off while under repair, the management offered an attractive lower rate.

To pay their way, Vertiline sold the items of value Mr. Mortlow had hidden with the confederate currency in the tin box he'd buried in the back yard: His watches, Abigale's jewelry, and some gold currency.

The incident at the bank had been the moment of discovery for both twins that each could affect the physical comfort and well-being of the other. Although the discovery disturbed Carolee, Mary found it wonderful.

***

Far from letting go of her flesh, Mary lay on the floor of her jail cell, feeling a stirring of a sexual desire as she reviewed memories of the spring of 1866.

While she and her twin were in the hospital, Carolee met the man she would later marry. Carolee's early encounters with Colonel Ambrose C. Marshall had informed the few sexual fantasies Mary had in life.

A hero of the South, convalescing at the hospital with a shoulder wound, the Colonel cut a tall, proud figure in Carolee's imagination, despite his underfed appearance. As Carolee spent time with the man alone, Mary was shocked and intrigued to find her twin developing passionate feelings for him.

Sheltered as they had been, with no mother throughout their adolescence, the twins knew nothing of sex. They might have learned something of it near the end of the war, when Union soldiers tried to molest them, but the Yankee dogs' efforts were thwarted and the twins rescued. Mary always did her best to push the memory aside whenever it occurred to her. The twins only became aware of the sexual nature of the attack after Carolee had sex with Colonel Marshall. Before that, the twins had thought making love to be merely hugging and kissing.

Memories of the sexual passion had formed a spark that settled between Mary's legs. With solid walls on three sides and no one in the corridor outside the door of her cell, she knew she wasn't being watched. She would hear if anyone approached her cell.

31

Well…Carolee watched, in her way. Though not as close as she'd been when confined in the same jail, Mary felt her twin's presence, knew that Carolee occupied a padded cell in some other building, somewhere. Seeing masturbation as a way to maintain interest in the flesh, she began to encourage Mary.

She let it be known that her twin's efforts dampened desire, and Carolee's presence retreated.

Mary shifted, trying to become more comfortable on the cold floor. *Please forgive me, Lord,* she thought as she reached for the spark and remembered.

Not long after Carolee met Colonel Marshall, she contrived to spend time with him in an unoccupied hospital room. Mary thrilled at the vicarious sensations as Carolee and the Colonel fell into bed together in the empty room, moaning and writhing together in the throes of their passion. Finally, after a bout of touching and kissing, Colonel Marshall spread Carolee's legs and forced his penis inside her.

Lying in her own hospital bed, mere yards away, the young Mary's enjoyment peaked with a euphoric sensation.

The fifty-nine-year-old Mary, lying on the jail cell floor touching herself, struggled to fan the sexual spark into full flame, but memory of Carolee's reaction on that day so long ago extinguished it entirely. Mary's hands dropped to her sides on the hard, clammy floor, and she struggled to catch her breath.

Carolee had screamed when Colonel Marshall penetrated her, then fought the man off. Although Mary knew something of what happened, she didn't get the full story from her sister until later. Apparently, several members of the hospital staff arrived in the room to find the Colonel cowering in a corner while Carolee struck him with a bedpan.

When Vertiline came to the hospital the next day and heard what had happened, she checked on Carolee's condition. Finding her largely unharmed, Vertiline left her sisters to speak with Colonel Marshall. She was gone for some time.

"She's going to punish us," Carolee whined.

"We're sixteen, all grown up," Mary said, although in truth she thought her twin was acting like an awful crybaby. "She won't spank you. What else can she do?"

When Vertiline returned, she described to the twins what Colonel Marshall had tried to do with Carolee and the purpose of it within the context of procreation. Carolee was horrified; Mary, fascinated.

"Colonel Marshall's family owns a sawmill in Tennessee," Vertiline said. "The business provides a good income. I insisted that to avoid disgrace and scandal, he should ask you to become his wife. When informed of the position our father held within the court, he asked several questions and saw the advantages to my proposal. He has agreed. I didn't tell him anything about our losses."

"No!" Carolee said. "I won't do it. You can't make me do it."

"I also told him that although the two of you would wed within the week, you would shortly thereafter travel to Virginia to train as an educator at Grandmother's college. I assured him that her college was second to none in the education of social graces and that it was the best investment one could make in the cultivation of a good wife. Many years will pass before you must share his bed."

"I will never allow him to do that again!" Carolee said, her face expressing disgust.

"That may be," Vertiline said patiently, "but for now, it is to our advantage to go through with the arrangement."

Mary knew Vertiline was right to insist on the marriage, not only on moral grounds, but for financial reasons as well. Silently, she agreed with Vertiline, knowing her twin was instantly aware of the assent.

"There will be a simple civil ceremony," Vertiline said to Carolee, "then you will remain in the hospital with your sister until we leave for Virginia in ten days."

Carolee could not stand up against both her sisters. Even so, Vertiline had only to endure the look in Carolee's eyes, while Mary could feel the hot, red burn of her twin's resentment. All their conflicts in life were petty by comparison. Mary taking Vertiline's side had set a wedge between the twins. Years would pass, however, before the resentment would seriously drive them apart. Although Mary did not regret her decision, she was sad to think that it resulted a loss of some love and trust between them.

Mary watched another cockroach enter her cell and crawl across the filthy floor. Carolee urged her to ignore the insect and try again for sexual release. Apparently the plan for stimulating the flesh with insect consumption had been abandoned in favor of the new idea.

She usually gets her way, Mary thought, *because God allows that she should.*

Since Carolee's choices often led to pain and destruction, Mary could not comprehend why the Lord tolerated them. But she had put herself in His loving hands long ago with the conviction that He knew best and that His ways were a mystery not always understood.

The cockroach struggled to climb the steel leg of the bunk securely bolted into the corner of Mary's cell. The slick metal presented little on which the insect might gain purchase and it fell several times. The uneven floor bit into Mary's back, but she took little notice of it as she watched the insect. Finally, the cockroach gave up and wandered away to inspect various crumbs of plaster that littered the floor.

About the same time, Carolee gave up on her badgering, at least for the moment, and Mary found she could relax.

Yes, Carolee usually gets her way, but not always.

Chapter 7
Vertiline—Denial

As the trial resumed in the afternoon, Vertiline tried to pay close attention to Mr. Hitchens's questioning of defense witnesses, but watching him only brought her more dread of taking the stand herself.

"Mr. Galbraith, when did Mrs. Carolee Mortlow Marshall first come to see you about her search for a property in New Jersey?" Mr. Hitchens asked.

Mr. Henry Galbraith was an attorney whose services Vertiline employed before her arrest. She knew Mr. Hitchens was trying to establish her alibi, but instead he created a muddle.

"Pardon me," Mr. Galbraith said, "but I have never met Mrs. Marshall. My dealings were with Miss Mortlow."

"I misspoke," Mr. Hitchens said. "Please accept my apology."

Vertiline's attorney had made several mistakes regarding the facts already, and Mr. Galbraith seemed disgusted and slightly embarrassed. She felt the same way, but if Mr. Hitchens made such mistakes while she was on the stand, the situation might be much worse. Her life hung in the balance.

To escape contemplating such eventualities as she waited her turn to testify, she allowed her mind to wander. She examined the countless dents and scratches on the surface of the defense table and wondered about those who had previously occupied her seat. She had a notion that those who were tormented with guilt for their crimes had expressed their restlessness and inner turmoil by scarring the table top while they waited to hear their fate. No doubt they had been found guilty of their crimes and were punished. Foolishly, she imagined that if she didn't contribute to the damage of the table, the jury would find her innocent. Although her hands were folded neatly in her lap, she thought of her father's reminder of table manners. "Mabel, Mabel, strong and able, keep your elbows off the table."

Don't worry, Father, she thought. *I wouldn't dare touch it.*

"Mr. Galbraith, when did you last see *Miss Vertiline Mortlow?*" Mr. Hitchens asked, pronouncing her name loudly.

She snapped out of her reverie upon hearing her name, and knew he was trying to draw her attention back to the task at hand.

I have no time for foolish notions, Vertiline thought. *I must pull myself together.*

"She was with me at my office from one o'clock to four o'clock in the afternoon of January 29th, 1906," Mr. Galbraith said.

"That's all for this witness, Your Honor," Mr. Hitchens said.

"Does the Prosecution wish to cross-examine the witness?" the judge grumbled. Mr. Tolland seemed an unhappy, angry sort of judge, so different from the Justice Vertiline's father had been.

"No, thank you, Your Honor," Mr. Kalinowski said.

"The witness may step down," the judge said. Although his eyes were clear, Mr. Tolland's skin had a slight yellow cast, suggesting he might have problems with his liver. Vertiline could easily picture him drinking heavily after hours.

Mr. Galbraith stepped away from the witness stand.

"Call the next defense witness," the judge said.

"The defense calls Miss Vertiline Mortlow," Mr. Hitchens said.

Vertiline rose slowly, was sworn in, and took her seat. Immediately, she regretted her decision to take the witness stand. Everyone stared in her direction, their scornful eyes darkening as they took her in. Many of those in the gallery were common folk from the street. Surrounded by the enemy, her Southern pride told her to look at them all with defiance.

No, I must not provoke them. I will look at them in a calm, dignified manner.

Despite her decision, Vertiline was surprised to find she couldn't look anyone squarely in the eye. She glanced about quickly, her eyes restless and trying to take in the whole scene without concentrating on the individual parts. With her short glimpse of the men of the jury, she'd found no compassion in their expressions.

But perhaps that was pure imagination. After all, they had yet to hear her speak.

The endless nights spent in a chilly cell, sleeping on a hard bunk, had taken their toll on her old joints. Hard and uncomfortable, the witness chair had been designed to make one squirm, the better to create an appearance of guilt under questioning. Despite the discomfort, she intended to remain still and poised, maintaining a proud posture. For the sake of her family, she must comport herself with dignity and acquit herself honorably.

After questioning Vertiline briefly about her past with an emphasis on her education and work as an educator, Mr. Hitchens changed his line of questioning. "Were you and your sisters aware that your niece, Mrs. Sneed, was addicted to narcotics?"

"No, we were not. She took laudanum for many years, but her doctor had given it to her. She had not been on the medication since before we left Brooklyn, nor during the two months we lived in East Orange."

"Could it be that Mrs. Orphia Sneed started taking the narcotic again to treat her depression?" Mr. Hitchens asked.

"Objection," Mr. Kalinowski said. "Council is speculating that Mrs. Sneed was suffering from melancholia."

Vertiline wondered what Mr. Hitchens was up to. He'd told her he would try to cast doubt on the prosecution's suggestion that Vertiline and her sisters provided the laudanum and used Orphia's addiction to it to control her. Perhaps that was it.

"Your Honor," Mr. Hitchens said, turning to the judge, "laudanum is a common narcotic preparation doctors provide for all kinds of good, including the treatment of depression, and is frequently found among a woman's personal effects."

"Sustained," the judge said.

Seemingly unfazed, Mr. Hitchens continued. "Your sister, Mrs. Mary Mortlow Sneed told investigators that her niece, Mrs. Orphia Sneed, was bedridden due to illness, that she had not been out of the house since moving to East Orange, and that she saw no doctor during that time. How could she have maintained such a habit without assistance if she didn't leave the apartment?"

Vertiline thought she understood her attorney's tactic. He was giving her an opportunity.

"Dr. Casby gave us all to understand that the medication was available only through a physician. I didn't know any differently until after I was arrested. Dr. Casby provided the medication to my niece, leaving it behind after his visits when we lived in Brooklyn. Perhaps she had enough left over to keep her supplied after we arrived in East Orange."

"Objection," Mr. Kalinowski said. "The idea that she had saved the laudanum for a rainy day is speculation on the witness's part."

Dr. Casby had testified the day before that he did not treat Orphia with laudanum. His indecency knew no bounds! Of course the depraved man would not admit giving the medication to Orphia, nor the true reason he did so. Vertiline would keep that ugly truth to herself, because her word against his would go nowhere, but at least the jury heard her say he'd provided the drug. They wouldn't forget, just as they would not forget his statement that laudanum was used to treat depression. That must have been what Mr. Hitchens had wanted. Perhaps her attorney was more clever than he appeared.

"Sustained," the judge grumbled.

"Just to be clear," Mr. Hitchens said, "I ask you now, were you aware at any point while your niece still lived that if she had been well enough to do so, she could have walked into the nearest druggist's and purchased laudanum herself?"

"No, I was not."

"Were you present at your East Orange basement apartment, located at 3550 Barns Street, at the time of Mrs. Orphia Marshall Sneed's death?"

"No."

"Where were you?"

"As Mr. Galbraith confirmed," she said, "I was meeting him at his office for business purposes at the time."

"Concerning the variety of suicide notes found in your correspondence folio in your bedroom in the basement apartment at the Barns Street address, who wrote those notes?"

"My niece," Vertiline said, "Mrs. Orphia Marshall Sneed." She wanted to say more, but her attorney had told her they must tread lightly on the subject because the expert witness's testimony was considered conclusive and anything she said to the contrary would be seen as self-serving.

With her last answer, Mr. Hitchens gave a satisfied smile, but Vertiline didn't know what he was so pleased about. He clearly didn't know the right questions to ask. While Mr. Galbraith's testimony confirmed Vertiline's alibi, and there was no way to prove that the sisters had caused Orphia to become addicted to laudanum, the prosecution's case didn't truly hinge on those issues. Their theory held that, regardless of how the addiction had come about, the three sisters conspired together to use Orphia's dread craving to isolate and control her after taking out the insurance policies. Once two years had passed—required before the policies would cover suicide—they drowned her in the tub to collect on the insurance payout. A difficult conspiracy to prove, but the prosecution had done their best to lead the jury to that conclusion by impugning the sisters' characters.

As she had several times since her arrest, Vertiline wished she could afford Mr. Galbraith instead of Mr. Hitchens.

As her attorney paused to consult his disorganized notes on the defense table, Vertiline again became aware that all eyes in the courtroom were on her. One fellow dressed in army fatigues, sitting in the front row of the gallery, seemed to snarl at her.

Vertiline cast about for somewhere to rest her gaze, a spot that would give her face and features a natural and dignified appearance to others, but where she would not discover yet another disapproving stare. To look at the floor would create a submissive appearance, while looking at the wall to the right or the ceiling would hurt her neck. Although the circular window above the entrance to the courtroom was too high to focus on for long, she looked up, hoping for a glimpse of blue sky. The clouds from earlier in the day had moved on, but the high humidity in the air caught the light of the sun and created a blinding whiteness.

As she felt her eyes watering from the brilliance, she quickly lowered her gaze. She would never forgive herself if she shed a tear in the court-room.

Looking down, she found the safe spot she'd been looking for: the railing behind the defense table. The woodwork stood significantly below the eye level of those in the first row of the gallery. Focusing on the pol-ished wood brought relief and a brief escape; the lathe-turned balusters supporting the rail looked so much like those of the stairway banister in her childhood home that for a moment, they took her there. Many memories of the house in which she'd grown up were pleasant, but not all of them.

Chapter 8
Vertiline—Adolescence

Vertiline hid in the dark at the top of the stairs in her house on Spring Street in Milledgeville, Georgia. Draped with two quilts and hugging the banister newel, she looked between the balusters as if through the bars of a cell, keeping her eyes on the entrance to the house downstairs. The front door was off its hinges and lay broken on the stoop. Freezing rain had given the pieces a clear, shiny coating that glistened in the moonlight. Vertiline knew she would never be able to put the door back together again.

General Sherman's Union forces, and the freed slaves following them, had moved through the area and left Milledgeville, all but a few remaining stragglers. Activity in the streets had died down and the neighborhood seemed deserted. Mr. Mortlow had kept vigil for so long and become so weak, he'd finally fallen asleep in his chair in the study, and had remained that way for days. They were all starving, and there was no food anywhere.

As if Vertiline could make it so by will alone, she imagined the house with its white walls, pale blue shutters, and gray slate roof gave an impression that it was totally abandoned and contained nothing of value. She imagined an invisible barrier in the doorway to keep the family safe. She tried to believe with conviction that no more Union soldiers or freed slaves would gain entrance to her home, and that her family had already seen the worst of the war. These were the thoughts of the seventeen-year-old girl.

Through recollection, the sixty-one-year-old Vertiline knew the power of the girl's imagination would not hold. The worst was yet to come.

No, I will not remember this!

Too late—before she could dash the memory entirely, Merrill appeared in the doorway.

Vertiline quickly took up another memory of the banister, one from when she was fourteen years old, on a day three months before the start of The War Between the States in 1861. Merrill, Mr. Mortlow's personal servant, posed no real threat in the recollection because Vertiline's father still lived.

On that day, Carolee and Mary had pushed the slave, Agnes, Merrill's wife, down the stairs. The woman broke her arm in the fall.

The twins excelled at creating household calamities such as setting fires, finding ways to trigger accidents involving hot food and drink in the kitchen and dining room, and breaking window glass and furniture to inflict minor injuries on those nearby. The household slaves suffered most from the mischief. The twins enjoyed stealing and destroying the clothing and other possessions of the slaves. Their more dangerous pranks occurred on or around the stairs in the center of the house. They dropped heavy objects from upstairs onto the heads of those passing through the hall below. By leaving on the treads slippery objects or items that rolled, such as croquet balls, the twins had sent several slaves tumbling headlong down the staircase.

Since the girls protected one another with silence, Vertiline had difficulty determining if one was the leader and the other merely followed or if both were equally culpable. In later years, she would come to suspect Carolee instigated most of the mischief, and Mary merely provided silent defense. They were an inseparable pair, and everyone knew it.

"My favorite child is the twins, Carolee and Mary, two halves of a whole," Mr. Mortlow had said more than once in Vertiline's presence. She didn't like to hear that. Carolee Calipash Mortlow and Mary Calipash Mortlow were insufferable brats. On the occasion Vertiline protested, he said, "But there are two of them. One person can't possibly compete. While Mary understands her mathematics, Carolee can draw and paint. Carolee can carry a tune and Mary is an excellent reader. Their middle name, Calipash, is passed down from our near-forgotten English forbears, an ancient and noble family. The legends say they had many twins among them, and that's why I gave your sisters the name. Given that Calipash twins have always been a bit notorious, I suppose Mary and Carolee's eccentricities are inevitable."

"Wouldn't I have the same blood?" Vertiline asked. "Should I be allowed such eccentricities?"

"No, dearest Vertiline," he said with a knowing smile and a chuckle. "Your sisters have their troubles too, and taken as individuals, they're not nearly as accomplished as are you. Without the guidance and example of their mother, they suffer a lack of discipline. As the eldest, you're their example."

Vertiline didn't ignore the duty implied by his words, but she didn't give the matter much thought either.

Although Agnes's fall occurred on an early Saturday morning when most still slept in bed, the sounds of the calamity and the poor woman's scream drew all within the house to the scene of the crime. Vertiline stepped from her bedroom and saw her sisters standing together, looking down the stairs. Being responsible for the accident, of course they would

41

not try to help. Vertiline brushed past the twins and joined her father and Merrill in the hall below. Merrill tried to help Agnes stand, but the small woman didn't respond. Agnes, her deep-set eyes and wide mouth drawn into a grimace, merely stared at the twins who still stood primly at the top of the stairs. The two blue-eyed brunette girls, twelve years old at the time, were in their lavender nightgowns. They looked much like Vertiline had at their age. Wide-eyed Carolee exhibited surprise and delight, while Mary seemed slightly troubled.

Vertiline thought her sisters had pulled another harmless prank until she saw the crooked line of Agnes's left forearm. Then her heart sank and she felt ill.

"Please tell us what happened," Mr. Mortlow said, but clearly he already knew. He looked up the stairs at the twins. Mary's face expressed an intense concentration for a moment, then she turned to her twin. Carolee pulled the grin back from her cheeks when Mary jabbed her with an elbow.

"I can't say, sir." Agnes said, her extreme expression withdrawn, but her misery evident beneath a veneer of stoicism. "I'm not at all certain what happened."

Merrill shook his head slowly as he examined Agnes's arm, his dark brow knotted up as if he were in pain. "If we don't take this in hand, Sir," he said to Mr. Mortlow in his deep, tumbling voice, "someone is liable to be killed one day."

"How dare you talk to Father like that," Vertiline said, her blood up and face suddenly hot. They were her sisters, and it was not his place. He deserved severe punishment. "You see, Father, because you've taken his advice in the past, he thinks he's your equal."

"Enough!" Mr. Mortlow said.

Although Merrill ducked his head and lowered his eyes, Vertiline hated him at that moment.

"It's not for you to say," Mr. Mortlow told her.

Vertiline had always been confused by her father's evident respect for Merrill. She'd seen Mr. Mortlow shake the black man's hand several times, and on one occasion she saw them embrace. Most of all, she resented that the black man had more of her father's ear than she did, but presently her thoughts returned to her sisters.

They should run and hide. Instead they continued to stand together; Mary shifting slowly from foot to foot, Carolee bouncing up and down with barely concealed excitement, looking down as if proud of what they'd done. They couldn't possibly understand the gravity of their offense.

Merrill lifted Agnes to her feet. "I'll take her to Jasper," he said. "He'll set her break."

"Bide a moment," Mr. Mortlow said, then he turned to Vertiline. "And *you* be still."

His stern features became set much the way they did on the few occasions she'd seen him considering a just punishment while performing his duties in court. He was about to hand out their punishment!

No, Father, not in front of Merrill, she mouthed, but the words didn't escape her lips. A terrible penalty was in store for the twins. The fact that they deserved it for the mistreatment of a slave would only compound the shame of the punishment. Tears would follow and the twins' unhappiness would grip the family for days to come. Vertiline would not endure it.

"I tripped her," she said. "Agnes was halfway down the stairs when I reached between the banister spindles and gripped her foot."

Merrill started to speak, but Mr. Mortlow waved him away, gesturing for silence, his expression severe. "You know better than to lie like that, Vert."

Carolee giggled, and Vertiline wanted to strangle both twins.

Well on her way to sharing her sister's punishment anyway, she pressed on. "Yes, but if I'm their example, I've failed and deserve the punishment. They're just little girls, Father. They don't understand, because I haven't done my duty as the eldest child well enough and shown them a better way."

Pride shone from Mr. Mortlow's warm, brown eyes, even as a sadness settled over his face. "Of course you're right. You're growing up so fast."

He turned to Merrill and Agnes. "Take her to Jasper. We'll have the doctor in later this afternoon."

Once the slaves had gone, Mr. Mortlow looked Vertiline in the eyes. He smiled gently. "You *are* the good example I hoped you'd be for your sisters. Your noble sacrifice for them is just what I'd expect. After your punishment, Ducy will no longer take charge of you girls. Instead, you'll become the woman of the house and make all decisions concerning your sisters."

The world around Vertiline grew soft and indistinct as the face of her father shone down on her like the warm sun on a perfect, cloudless day. Her heart leapt gently in her chest and she took short, sweet breaths, savoring the moment of her triumph.

"But your punishment must be severe." His head tilted to one side and the sadness returned to his face. "You will room with Ducy and the other female slaves for a month."

A joke surely—no other explanation was possible.

"You'll share their food and their duties," he continued.

No, it was not a joke. His face no longer shone brightly. His features were set again.

The world around Vertiline grew dark.

"No one outside the household will know of it. You'll bear it with as much grace as possible. I'll make sure your sisters are watching."

The darkness closed in.

"Vert, are you listening to me?

Mr. Mortlow's voice and image receded.

"Vertiline Gertrude Mortlow, you will pay attention to your father!"

She felt the cold floor against her cheek as the darkness rolled over her like a shroud.

"Vert!"

She gratefully embraced the darkness and let go with the erroneous belief that sudden death had saved her from a terrible fate.

❦

Far from dead, Vertiline awoke lying on a straw mattress. A dark brown hand, with pale finger tips and palm, lifted a cool, damp rag from her forehead. The hand belonged to her old slave governess, Ducy, who sat on the edge of the bed. The old woman's eyes, brown with gray edges, were focused on shadows across the room, her broad open face untroubled, but weary. Since her hair had become too thin to keep her head warm, Ducy had taken to wearing a cap she'd knitted from pale blue cotton.

"Where am I?" Vertiline asked, glancing around, but she knew without an answer. She had been in the female slaves' quarters on rare occasions. Each time, she'd experienced what she called a sinking spell, a moment of nausea brought on by a clash of fear, revulsion, and an unaccountable sadness. The room held nothing to provide it with character. The walls had been coated with an unattractive mix of colors left over from several painting projects around the house, including a pale green, a mauve, a thin yellow, and a dusty pink. Where they came together, the hues created ugly grays and browns. Three windows up near the ceiling, too small to climb through, provided only a glimpse of the top of the house next door, a view largely obscured by the foliage of several trees. The floorboards looked like they had never been polished, and the furniture was of poor quality. The coarseness of the gray bedding beneath her, and a smell of body odor and old age that hung in the air, spoke in dark tones to Vertiline of a grim reality: The slaves suffered a cruel lot in life with virtually no rewards.

"I won't stay here," Vertiline said, sitting up and looking toward the closed door.

"Your father knew you'd need time to warm to the idea," Ducy said.

Vertiline leapt toward the door and found it locked. She pounded on it with her fists and cried out for her father.

Ducy said something, but the deafening noise Vertiline was making prevented her from hearing the governess.

No one came to let Vertiline out. Perhaps they had all left, abandoning her in the dungeon.

In the shadows to the left, Vertiline could see Ducy silent and motionless on the bed.

"You are a stupid old woman," Vertiline said, facing the door. "You can't keep me here."

"It's not up to me, Vert."

"Don't call me that, you smelly creature." Vertiline didn't like what had come out of her mouth, but since the words had been spoken, she had to justify them. "You don't know your place. Only family and friends call me that. Don't dare pretend you're *good enough* to call me that."

"You let me use it before, Miss," Ducy said quietly, without inflection.

"Don't talk back to me." Vertiline swung around and glared at the slave, then turned back to the door and pounded again. "I shouldn't be in this filthy room," she cried.

"That's right, Miss."

"How can you stand it? Where's your pride?"

"It's not up to me, Miss. I do what I can with what's provided. Now, you must do the same."

Vertiline turned, advanced swiftly on Ducy, and struck her in the face. Vertiline was astonished and horrified by her own actions. Still, while her governess kept her eyes focused on the floor, Vertiline struck her repeatedly as tears of frustration sprang from her eyes. Little need did the old woman have to defend herself, for after the first shocking blow, the strength had drained from the girl, yet clearly Ducy absorbed a punishment Vertiline meant for herself. Soon the girl's tears had more power than her fists. She stumbled back, fell into the corner by the door, and curled into a ball.

Hot tears flowed freely for over an hour. Vertiline's mouth tasted of salt and iron. The front of her blouse became soaked through, creating a clammy chill, and her throat hurt. The heels and balls of her hands had become bruised and sore from striking the door.

Throughout the emotional display, Ducy had remained silent and still, seated on the edge of the straw bed, dimly illuminated on one side by the green, leaf-filtered light from the high windows.

Finally Vertiline stood and allowed herself to imagine the coming month. She swallowed painfully a couple of times and began to quake from fear.

Having nowhere else to go, she stumbled toward her slave governess. Ducy looked up. Their eyes met and a quiet filled the room.

Per the common wisdom of Vertiline's community and Church, and the prevailing attitudes of her schoolmates, she had always maintained emotional distance from all slaves. Still, Ducy represented stability and comfort. She'd soothed Vertiline in illness, provided guidance in interpreting Mr. Mortlow's complex world, and, despite much mistreatment and a hard life, had many times given a kind word to Vertiline when she truly needed one.

She took a step toward Ducy and fell into her arms. The shame of the moment fled when the old woman embraced her.

"There, there, now, Miss," Ducy said. "Your father hasn't abandoned you. He's offering you something grand. I'm to teach you all you'll need to know to run the house."

"But I am his daughter, not—"

"Yes, but to assume the responsibility, to exercise such *power* over your *sisters*, you must start from scratch and learn everything." Ducy had smiled with the emphasized words, a look of mischief in her eyes. "You're too young to be the woman of the house without experience. When your mother passed away and I had to take care of everything—your father, you girls, the servants, and house—it was almost more than I could bear. I had to learn, and that's just what you'll do. I'm too old to keep it up. The time has come early for you, but you'll put away childish concerns and become a woman now." Ducy made the statement with such confidence, Vertiline couldn't help but believe her.

A slight smile lifted one corner of Vertiline's mouth. To have power over her sisters and to be in charge of herself—what would that mean? Remembering the twins standing proudly at the top of the stairs earlier, she wanted them to suffer. If she were in charge, they'd receive a good spanking. The horrid brats were responsible for the predicament in which she found herself. But then maybe Vertiline wasn't in such a bad spot after all.

"You girls have given me a hard time for many a year," Ducy said. "But you listen to me for a solid month and you'll be ready."

With the kind treatment Vertiline was receiving, she felt bad for all the mean things she'd said and done to Ducy growing up. Vertiline participated at times with her sisters in pranks, but had never physically hurt the woman before that day.

"I'm sorry I hit you," she said.

Ducy shrugged and produced a sad smile. As Vertiline watched, the old woman's expression gradually changed to a happy smile with sparkling eyes. "When you're ready, your father will allow me to retire." She let out a long sigh. "These bones are ready to sit down and stay seated for a while. I look forward to a time when I can watch the madness of this house without a care in my head."

Vertiline could not help smiling to see Ducy grin so large.

From the direction of the door, came the sound of a key turning in the lock.

∼⚬∼

The training took two months, but after the first thirty days, Vertiline was allowed to return to her own bed, in her own bedroom, and to eat with the family again. Successfully trained, she became the woman of the house at age fourteen.

Carolee referred to her as "Slave Vertiline" throughout her training. The twins—again she didn't know which one—tripped Vertiline on the stairs. She caught herself on the banister, preventing herself from falling headlong into the hall below. She looked to see who was responsible. Mary was the closest, but Carolee giggled not far away. At twelve years of age, instead of maturing, the twins were more childish than ever before.

She learned to organize the meals, the shopping, the schedules and methods of laundry and house cleaning, the protocols for receiving and entertaining guests, and dealing with the various local businesses that provided services to the household.

Ducy also passed on to her the protocols for discipline Mr. Mortlow had established for the governess. Vertiline found them insufficient, and a week after she achieved her new status and station, she broke from her father's procedures to prove her authority over her sisters. She evacuated the female slave quarters one day when Mr. Mortlow was away on business for the court. She closed the shutters outside the windows of the room to darken the interior and then locked Mary in the chamber for most of a day. Mary cried and pounded on the door much the way her big sister had, and Vertiline grimaced as she thought of Mary's distress.

Ducy watched the drama in the house unfold from her new rocking chair. She didn't once lift a finger to help, but smiled gently to see Vertiline's discomfort. Unladylike, the woman of the house stuck her tongue out at the old slave.

After an hour or so, Mary became quiet.

Delighted with her twin's punishment, Carolee played with two cloth dolls in the hall outside the room. She spoke to one of them as if it were Mary. "So dangerous to trip your sister on the stairs," Carolee said in mocking tones, her voice loud enough for Mary to hear through the door. "You might have broken *her* arm too. You've been very bad indeed, Mary, and now we have to turn you into a slave."

The woman of the house told her to stop teasing her sister and Carolee became quiet—too quiet. Later, Vertiline discovered that Carolee had gone upstairs, taken a bottle of ink from Mr. Mortlow's study, and used the liquid to dye one of her dolls black.

Carolee didn't know her big sister made ready to punish her as well. Vertiline had prepared makeshift beds for the female slaves in the carriage house and stoked up an old stove there to provide heat against the coming chilly March night.

When allowed to leave the female slave quarters, Mary was first greeted with a gloating Carolee who held out the two dolls, one black and one white. Vertiline snatched the dolls away, shoved Carolee in the room, slammed the door shut, and turned the key in the lock.

She wailed and shouted relentlessly. "Vertiline's a curryscat!" she yelled. "When I get out I'll hexspecks your hair! I'll put good-gollymallolly in your shoes."

Confused, Vertiline looked to Mary for an explanation.

"Carolee makes up curse words for us to use," she said. "We can say them and not get in trouble. Curryscat is a dog that eats its stool. Hexspecks is when you save what comes out when you blow your nose to put on someone. I'm not sure about the last one. Sounds like the one about diarrhea. You'd better look in your shoes before you put them on."

Carolee kept up the tirade. She was fortunate her father wasn't home. He would not have tolerated such outbursts and would have punished her further. That night, Vertiline could not sleep in the house with all of Carolee's noise, as her shouting and banging on walls and doors continued sporadically on into the evening. Vertiline prepared two more beds in the carriage house and slept there with Ducy and the other female slaves. The woman of the house was no longer above sleeping with them, but Mary wouldn't hold with it. She stayed in the hall near her twin, and in the morning looked as if she hadn't slept a wink.

Vertiline assembled all the household servants in the hall outside the female slave quarters in preparation for releasing her sister. When finally allowed to leave the room, Carolee's fists were black and blue, her eyes rimmed red and swollen nearly shut. Vertiline returned the two dolls to the girl—both dyed black. Defeated, Carolee hung her head and went upstairs to her room.

Ever after that, for the slightest infraction of Vertiline's rules, the twins suffered punishment, and there was no further question of her authority.

While she enjoyed a few victories, Vertiline became the woman of the house at the worst possible moment. Within a month of assuming the role, during which she planned her first garden party, The War Between the States began. Of the forty-five people she invited to the party—over thirty of whom were young adults, including twenty-five men with good prospects—only twelve people responded to her invitation. Nearly all the young men had signed up to fight in the conflict. Vertiline spent the afternoon of the party dutifully talking with friends of her parents, and everyone went home by sunset. The Chinese lanterns weren't lit and the year was too young, the nights still too cold, for lightning bugs.

Adulthood wasn't what she'd expected. The absurd war had spoiled everything.

Chapter 9
Carolee—Miserable Creature

In what little contact she had with the staff of the sanatorium, Carolee gave an impression that she was stuporous. She offered nothing else in interactions with others. Because she'd given one of the bailiffs a bloody nose, she was confined to a padded cell most of the time and had little to occupy her mind within her surroundings.

Yet her own situation matter little to her at present. She fumed and brooded over her failure to reignite her twin's desire to live. Somehow, Mary had learned to ignore her twin's presence in her mind, a new development which could not stand if they were to continue.

Carolee shouted, cursed, and called her sister names. She beat herself against the padded walls of her cell. She teased Mary about the future she would have without her. Carolee pinched herself painfully and pulled her own hair out by the roots. As her efforts escalated, she relived the history of her deepest anger toward her twin, knowing that Mary couldn't entirely avoid awareness of the recollections and their attendant emotions. Carolee's resentment toward her twin flowed from Mary's agreement with Vertiline that Carolee should wed Colonel Ambrose C. Marshall.

I would never have betrayed Mary like that. As far as Carolee was concerned, the breach of trust had led to all the suffering that followed, including their present predicament.

⁓✦⁓

The most dreadful episode with Colonel Marshall would not come for many years after their hasty marriage, for he returned to his family in Tennessee and Carolee moved with her sisters to live with their grandmother, Winifred Sobearn. The three young women lived in Winifred's home on the small campus of the school she had owned and run for twenty-two years, the Montcomber Female College in Christiansboro, Virginia. The campus consisted of ten acres with five tidy buildings; a two-story brick schoolhouse that held classrooms and a dining hall, two Italianate clapboard structures—one being the Sobearn family home and the other a larger house serving as a dormitory—a rustic wooden cottage that was the old Sobearn home, currently used for storage, and a neglected carriage house and stable. Including Winifred, the college had eight female teachers of various ages, a maintenance man, and a young woman who served as housekeeper and cook. Fifty to seventy-five students lived and studied at the academy at any given time. As each of the sisters in turn completed their education at the school, their grandmother rewarded them with a place on her staff. By 1872 all three had become educators at the Montcomber Female College.

Carolee walked into the middle of a conversation between Vertiline and her grandmother, Winifred, during an afternoon tea in the parlor of the Sobearn house. The two sat somewhat stiffly at opposite ends of the settee.

"What is the name of the young man to whom Mary is betrothed?" Winifred asked, then she noticed Carolee and a smile appeared among the deep wrinkles of her face. "Please sit, dear, and have some tea."

"His name is Frederick Sneed," Vertiline said. "You met him last week."

"Thank you, Grandmother." Carolee sat on the pastel green and coral silk of an upholstered chair that was part of an ugly set of French Provincial furniture dominating the parlor. She poured herself a cup of tea, and, although hungry—she was always hungry and fought the pangs off daily to keep from becoming fat—she chose not to take a ginger snap for fear that while biting into the crisp cookie, she might miss a word or two of the conversation.

"Yes, yes, I remember," Winifred said with a slight wave of her knobby, arthritic hand, but clearly she didn't.

"Do you remember where we were when you met him?" Vertiline asked. She frequently tested Winifred's memory, which seemed to become worse by the day.

Although obviously irritated with the question, Winifred remained quiet for some time, perhaps trying to find the correct answer. Carolee watched the crepe paper and parchment skin of the old woman's neck pulsate with the movement of blood through the vessels beneath.

"Grandmother doesn't like me," Vertiline had told her sisters two months ago, "but she loves you two. Most of her thoughts are fleeting, but wanting to be a great-grandmother before she dies persists. Since Colonel Marshall's mill has not been a successful enterprise, Grandmother is our greatest benefactor. To ensure that we earn the greater portion of her estate, we must create the loving families she will want to cherish and support. Maintaining her beneficence is our greatest hope for continued prosperity."

Carolee understood the fear behind her older sister's words; no matter what the costs, they must avoid a future that would lead to the kind of poverty and degradation they'd experienced during and shortly after the war.

"The only way we have to compete with Aunt Eleanor for Winifred's estate is for you two to bear offspring," Vertiline concluded.

Carolee knew that Vertiline destroyed any correspondence between Winifred and her daughter, their spinster Aunt Eleanor, who had removed to California some twenty years earlier.

Carolee offered a nod of affirmation. "I will write to Mr. Marshall about a visit," she said, but had no intention of doing so.

Mary responded enthusiastically, and that very day began the search for a spouse. Within a month, she'd met Frederick Sneed and he'd proposed.

Winifred seemed to pop up out of her thoughts, her wet, green eyes hopeful. "The church picnic! He was the man who spoke of *Sunday bullets.*"

"Yes," Vertiline said. "You thought that very humorous, didn't you?"

Perhaps the obsequious tone Vertiline always took with their grandmother was what Winifred didn't like. Carolee first noticed the affected voice shortly after they came to live in Virginia in early summer of 1866. "Why do you sound so…unreasonably pleasant?" she had asked.

"I want her to believe we love her more than anything in the world," Vertiline had explained.

Winifred chuckled. "Yes, he was very funny." A look of relief and triumph brightened her weathered face. "He said folks always saved the worst of their crops to share at Sunday picnics. They were *awful* peas. Might've made better bullets after all. I nearly embarrassed myself laughing so hard."

Carolee smiled, remembering the disapproving looks from the other members of the church who didn't know what inspired the laughter.

"I can't remember what he looks like," Winifred said with a sad smile that disappeared abruptly. She shrugged. "One of the costs of living to a ripe, old age is having difficulty with one's memory, but it's distressing nonetheless."

"Yes, Grandmother," Vertiline said, "making it all the more important to have your wishes known before it's too late. If you'd like to go over your will with me, I'm happy to help."

"I have already written my will. It's done." Winifred looked away, pretending to consider the view outside the window to her right. In profile, she looked birdlike. Most of her features had withered except her nose, which had become something of a beak.

"Yes," Vertiline said, "but things change. With Mary getting married and having children, and Carolee traveling soon to see her husband with the expressed purpose of starting their family, you may want to reconsider some of your decisions."

Winifred smiled, but said nothing and continued to look out the window.

"Can you tell me about the financial worth of the school?" Vertiline asked.

"Let's talk about something more pleasant than business and wills," Winifred said, glancing at Vertiline with barely disguised mistrust.

"You know my sisters and I will stay on to continue your legacy." Vertiline turned to look her grandmother in the eye. "With that in mind, it's in our best interest and yours that we know your wishes."

Carolee liked that Vertiline kept at it.

Winifred took a deep breath and exhaled suddenly. "I don't want you three to have the burden of the school." She frowned slightly. "Rest assured, I've thought of you girls and your children. That's all I'll say."

Carolee was disappointed to realize that her older sister had pushed a little too hard. Still, Carolee would not know how to pursue their interests with Winifred, and had to trust Vertiline to do the job.

With Winifred's response, Vertiline immediately became silent and sat up straight to present the most proper posture. At the age of twenty-five years, she wasn't a handsome woman by any stretch of the imagination. Carolee could not remember a time when a man had shown any interest in Vertiline. She was somewhat taller than the average woman, and had strong features, a long nose like their father, deep-set blue eyes, a high forehead, and a firm, slightly cleft chin. But perhaps appearance had little to do with the lack of romantic interest. Vertiline had a stone-cold serious aspect to her personality that Carolee found compelling in a leader, but she suspected men found intimidating.

Concerning Winifred's will, Carolee knew that despite Vertiline's current silence, she would not let the matter go. Clearly Winifred disliked Vertiline for the very reasons Carolee considered her the perfect ally—Vertiline was dogged in pursuit of their interests.

Nearly a year later, Carolee had rapped Edna Munro on the crown of her head for the fifth time—the young woman was incapable of sitting up straight with hands folded in her lap—when Vertiline opened the door to the classroom and stood at the threshold looking in. The class would not end for another ten minutes, but her demeanor suggested impatience. Carolee continued to walk among the students with her ruler in plain view.

Seeing Vertiline, Mary, who led the class, stood and cleared her throat. "That's enough, Felicia," she said. The girl was reading from a collection of American poetry, but she stopped in mid-verse. Mary turned to the young woman seated nearest the door. "Nora, please take charge of the class."

Nora wore the red collar that designated her as a member of the disciplinary committee, a group Carolee had started to help maintain order in the classrooms and dormitory. The committee system took advantage of the desire for power among some students and fear from all the rest, but the structure helped take some of the pressure off the staff.

Nora rose with a self-satisfied smirk and took Mary's position at the head of the class.

Carolee handed Nora her ruler, followed Mary into the hall outside the classroom, and shut the door behind her. The sharp sounds of the door closing and the catch springing into place echoed down the hall as the sisters huddled together and Vertiline began to speak in hushed tones.

"I have good news. Today, I was going through Grandmother's armoire and found her will. She'd hidden it in the right sleeve of the dress she'd asked to wear at her funeral. Grandmother leaves us money, half of what she has left, which probably doesn't amount to much. The other half goes to Aunt Eleanor. I have asked Mr. Harold Yates for permission to view the ledger for the school's finances several times." She referred to the man Winifred employed as a bookkeeper. "He will not allow it. I'll keep trying and hope he doesn't talk about my request with Grandmother. Even if he does, she's not likely to remember it for long."

Good news? Carolee could only see cause for concern.

Vertiline paused, then began again with a grim face. "Grandmother intends the college to be sold after her death, with whatever profits made from the sale going to an old soldiers' home that houses disabled veterans from both the Confederate *and* Union armies."

Carolee could feel her blood rising in anger, and Vertiline continued in a manner that helped express those feelings. "We will not go hungry while our family's money feeds and shelters Yankees," she said, shaking her head slowly, her features grim.

The fierce look in Vertiline's eyes, though wonderful, only served to deepen Carolee's concern.

"What can we do?" Mary asked. "Is she so mad she doesn't honor what divine providence decrees? Can she no longer discern who is deserving and who is not?"

Carolee had seen Winifred's mental decline accelerate rapidly over the past few months. The old woman was nearly dead. Her estate would be a picked-over carcass if they didn't act.

"You told us there was *good news*," Carolee said.

"Yes," Vertiline said, then paused with a slight grin.

"*What is it?*" Mary and Carolee asked in unison.

"I took care of it," Vertiline said. "It's done!" Her smile grew so large as to become frightening. "The document was handwritten. Her handwriting is just what she taught us, no more, no less. With that and the practice I've had signing for her, it was an easy matter to create a new one that appears to have her signature. I removed all reference to the old soldiers' home and Aunt Eleanor. In her condition, if she reads it, she's unlikely to remember what she originally intended."

Mary nodded her approval, her face bearing a smile that Carolee knew mirrored her own.

Now the sisters would gain the choicest morsels. Carolee's mouth watered. Her allegiance to Vertiline was absolute.

~~~✣~~~

Mary and Frederick Sneed married in 1874. They had two sons over the next two years, James, born in 1875 and Fletcher in 1876. Frederick had inherited his father's hardware business and a beautiful home close to town in Christiansboro. Because Mary had duties at the college, however, she rarely spent time at home and kept a room in the Sobearn house.

Carolee had successfully avoided seeing Colonel Marshall since shortly after marrying him. She received one letter from him in 1876. In it, he asked that she join him in Tennessee, and she responded to the letter with a false promise to do so once Winifred felt better. With her grandmother's worsening dementia, the pressure from Vertiline for Carolee to bear children diminished.

In 1877, at eighty-nine years of age, Winifred stepped down as headmistress of the college. Vertiline took up the position.

As far as Carolee was concerned, her grandmother's life wasn't worth living. Winifred had become incontinent and refused to bathe on her own. She no longer tolerated her dentures, and her food was prepared so she could swallow it without chewing. For all her problems, however, she could still get around on her feet. On occasion, a search party formed to locate her somewhere on the property and lead her back to the house. Within a short time after her retirement, Winifred's mind became that of a petulant child.

Most of her care fell to Carolee, as Vertiline spent the bulk of her time on headmistress duties, and Mary busied herself taking care of her two young boys. Carolee became increasingly disgusted with the old woman, yet couldn't help but remember the times Winifred had been a loving grandmother, doting on the twins, providing them with special treats, and plenty of kind and tolerant attention.

As time passed, Winifred became mistrustful of those around her. One day, while Carolee smoothed her grandmother's white hair with a fine silver hairbrush, Winifred turned and struck her in the face with an arthritic, clawed hand.

"You brush *too hard!*" she cried.

"I'm sorry, Grandmother," Carolee said automatically. She wiped away blood that welled up from fingernail scratches in her cheek. "I'll go slower, but I must get the tangles out. With all the time you spend in bed—"

"Doesn't matter how much I sleep. You pull hard because you want hair to make one of those dreadful memorials. You and your sisters can't wait until I'm gone. You're already planning, plotting…planting." Winifred had already forgotten what upset her. She chuckled. "Almost time to plant peas." She paused with a big smile, then said, "Sunday bullets!"

Wanting to bash Winifred's head in, Carolee quickly set the heavy brush down to keep from using it as a weapon.

The times when Winifred became insolent and belligerent came more frequently. If Carolee had believed in God, she'd have asked him to take her grandmother away to Heaven or Hell—she didn't care which.

A few months later, in 1879, while hurrying up the stairs of the house, Carolee broke one of the brass stair rods that held the runner down, and the rug sagged over the riser. She thought back to her childhood pranks on the slaves and imagined what might happen if Winifred came upon the loose runner unawares. Carolee decided to ignore the danger and remain silent about the condition of the rug.

She didn't see her grandmother's fall, but Carolee wondered if she'd have enjoyed watching the old crone take the tumble down the stairs. She heard that her older sister had discovered Winifred lying helpless at the foot of the staircase. Vertiline called on the maintenance man, Joshua Webbert, to carry the old woman to her bed. The family doctor, Samuel Claytor, did little for Winifred and she passed away the next morning.

At the funeral, Carolee stood beside the grave after everyone left, wondering why she didn't feel anything for the loss of her grandmother. The common response of grieving seemed appropriate, yet even the fondest memories involving Winifred in happier times, the holidays, birthdays, special meals and events in which their grandmother made the twins the center of her world, weren't the least bit wistful. Instead, she felt giddy, and had been trying to hide the feeling from those around her all day.

Turning to leave the cemetery, she discovered Mary standing beside her. The two women looked so much alike that to see her sister was to see herself, but Carolee paused for a moment to consider her appearance in the *sister-mirror*, looking for evidence of the missing grief. Mary's eyes were almond-shaped, blue, and lacked a certain warmth, humor perhaps. They showed no grief. Mary's dark brown hair, worn much the way Carolee wore her own, was pulled back and secured with modest pins at the back of her head. Sober and intelligent in appearance, Mary's pale, round face had a high forehead, the long, straight Mortlow nose, and a small mouth held so primly that it had little more color than the rest of her face. Not one of Cupid's most powerful weapons, the thin bow of her lips opened to speak even as Carolee focused on them. "She displeased the Lord in some way, and he struck her with madness," Mary said. "You've done nothing he didn't want you to do."

The fact that Mary was aware of her twin's role in Winifred's death was exhilarating to Carolee. The idea that God had used her as His instrument, however, was foolishness. That she had taken a human life and suffered no repercussions seemed proof that there was no God. If the twins' unspoken pact to protect one another with silence held, there would never be any consequences.

Two days after the funeral, Carolee walked in on an argument in the parlor of the Sobearn house between Vertiline and Mary. Although the two women sat properly on the settee, spoke in hushed tones, and were measured in their attitudes toward one another, the battle of recriminations they waged spoke of an anger barely contained. The emotion wasn't nearly as disturbing as their apparent great need to control it. Carolee had rarely seen Mary and Vertiline at such odds. Something was terribly wrong.

"You should have known about this," Mary said, her left hand tightening into a fist around the papers it held. She wasn't looking at her older sister.

"How could I?" Vertiline asked. Her lips, pressed into a hard line, barely moved. "The old woman wouldn't even speak to me toward the end."

"You pretended you had everything in hand, that you were in charge." Mary said, cutting her eyes at her older sister with a glint of mistrust.

"I depended on *you*," Vertiline said. "You're the one with the head for figures and Grandmother loved you. You talked to her more than anyone. You said you'd drawn her out and that nothing was amiss."

Although reluctant to get involved, Carolee knew that whatever calamity had befallen the family affected her as well. Finally she asked, "What has you two so upset?"

Mary turned, her face a frightful mask of self-control. "The incorporated business of the college is heavily in debt. That's why Grandmother didn't want to leave it to us. She was protecting us."

Carolee *did not* have a head for figures, but she certainly took the enormity of Mary's distress seriously. Her twin rarely displayed strong emotion. Carolee felt herself trembling slightly as she questioned her faith in Vertiline's decision-making. However the older sister might try to deflect responsibility, there was no doubt she was in charge and had failed the twins.

"The school will eventually have to declare bankruptcy," Vertiline said stiffly. "The debt is just too great. Before that happens, we'll draw off funds and secrete them into another account. We must make the failure of the college appear natural, and plan to be gone before anyone discovers the truth."

Again Carolee knew little about such things, but she suspected there were many ways of being caught and punished for stealing from the college. When Carolee stole from others, the act was always simple and rarely was she in danger of being caught. She was only discouraged from committing a theft when the possible consequences outweighed the value of the thing Carolee wanted to take.

She looked for her twin's reaction to Vertiline's words.

Mary exhaled heavily. Uncharacteristically, she slouched for a moment in defeat. Then she sat up straight, looked Vertiline in the eye, nodded curtly, and said, "I'll find a way."

Carolee found her twin's reaction somewhat reassuring, but perhaps they both had been misguided in their belief that their older sister could protect them from the dangers of the world. Was it possible that Vertiline was merely older and not wiser than the twins?

Carolee found no ready answers for the question. She preferred to depend on a strong leader because she knew she couldn't survive on her own. She also knew Mary felt the same way, even now. Carolee was left despairing and insecure in a swiftly changing world.

The board of trustees of the Montcomber Female College had the responsibility to oversee the school's policies concerning students and curriculum, while business, staff, and financial matters had been the exclusive territory of Winifred Sobearn. With her death, the responsibility fell to Vertiline Mortlow. She dismissed three of the teachers, the maintenance man, the young housekeeper, and the cook. The sisters worked harder to compensate. Vertiline also let go of Winifred's bookkeeper and gave Mary the position.

Colonel Marshall wrote again in 1880:

My dear wife,

I hope you are well and this letter finds you in good spirits, surrounded by the loving grace of your family and that of the good Lord Himself.

I am in good physical health, but my spirits have been rendered unhappy by present circumstance.

I have not received a letter from you and can only believe this is a reflection of our shared disappointment in the progress of the sawmill. I vowed that I would not be a burden to you and would withhold correspondence until I had made a success of the business, but as you know, I broke that vow with my letter of four years ago. I was lonely and sent it in a moment of weakness. I hope you can forgive me.

It is well that you did not join me, as my situation has only worsened. I will not bore you with business for which you should have no interest, but will only say that the struggle here has been against northern businessmen with monopolistic designs on the industry. Washington passes legislation to aid them in their efforts. An honest Southern businessman without significant financial help cannot hope to prosper. Whether I will one day succeed is hidden in the future. I cannot expect you to suffer with me until the time of such revelation.

Despite financial difficulties, I have religiously paid into a ten-thousand dollar life insurance policy for which you are the beneficiary. If I must declare bankruptcy, I will not be able to afford to pay the premium. This is the one thing of value I have been able to maintain and may be all my future has to offer you. If you believe it is worthwhile to continue these payments, please consider whether your assistance, or that of your family, in paying the premium is justified. Although the monthly payment is small, holding that in reserve to help pay expenses on the mill would allow me to pursue the dream a little longer. That may be all it will take.

Your husband in perseverance,
Colonel Ambrose C. Marshall

Carolee gratefully accepted when Vertiline offered to respond to Colonel Marshall's letter. "Please do not tell him that Grandmother has passed away," Carolee said.

An unwelcome surprise came six months later, in the fall of 1880, when the Colonel arrived at the Montcomber Female College with everything he owned stuffed into a trunk and two ragged portmanteaus. The man Colonel Marshall had hired to drive him to the college from the train station had turned his buckboard around and was already a hundred yards down the drive by the time Carolee knew of her husband's arrival. Otherwise, she would have demanded to have the Colonel driven back to the station right away.

"Good day, Mrs. Marshall, Miss Mortlow," he said, making only brief eye contact.

Carolee tried to silently communicate her discomfort to her older sister as they stood in the entrance to the Sobearn house. Vertiline didn't seem to notice. She gestured toward the door and said, "Colonel, please come in."

After using the boot scrape beside the front door, he began to haul his belongings into the foyer of the Sobearn house. The difficulty Colonel Marshall had handling the trunk indicated he'd lost some of the muscle he'd had as a soldier, but he still looked powerful. His posture was not as tall and proud as before, and his long face held lines that spoke of frequent worry.

Vertiline led him to the parlor. "Please be seated, Colonel Marshall," she said. "I must speak with your wife for a moment."

He seemed somewhat confused, but nodded his approval.

Carolee and Vertiline left him sitting in the parlor while they had a private conversation in the kitchen, sitting at the table.

"He wrote to say he was forced to file for bankruptcy on the sawmill," Vertiline whispered. "Since I was handling your correspondence with him, I told him to come here."

Carolee allowed her outrage to show on her face.

Vertiline looked at her squarely. "He has the insurance policy, and Mary and I decided to continue his payments when he was unable. *You* are the beneficiary."

"Then he should die this very day." The tension around Carolee's eyes and mouth grew unbearably tight and painful.

"Don't be absurd. And keep your voice down." Vertiline shook her head in disgust. "We haven't been able to afford to hire anyone to perform maintenance on the buildings. Now we'll have free labor. He's been beaten down. We'll build him back up a little and work him hard, and if he dies, we'll gain from that too."

Carolee shook with fury. If she'd been willing to take charge of the correspondence with her husband, he wouldn't have come. Since decisions made while angry often led to more pain, however, she struggled to let the feelings go and accept the appalling product of Vertiline's judgment.

"I'll have a talk with Colonel Marshall," Vertiline said. "Don't be concerned about your duties to him. If you make the effort, you should be able to get the upper hand."

When they returned to the parlor, the Colonel was slumped in his chair looking small, broken, and pitiful. Carolee easily read his character. Vertiline had been right about him.

The sisters each took a seat on the settee.

"Colonel Marshall," Vertiline said, and he looked up as if he hadn't heard them come in the room. "Carolee has been independent for a long time. Your marriage and your feelings for each other never had a chance to develop. That will take time."

"Yes, miss," he said. "All that is true, and I don't expect much."

"Please allow for some time to pass before insisting on sexual intercourse," Vertiline said.

At these words, Carolee's chagrin was eclipsed by the display of Colonel Marshall's embarrassment. His eyes became wide and he let out a short gasp. He turned away and took several deep breaths before turning back.

"Yes, miss," he said. "I will be lucky if she ever feels anything for me. I have not performed well in this world since the war." He glanced timidly at Carolee.

She took advantage of his distress to give him a hard stare, and he turned away again. His reaction seemed to open a window onto a possible future for Carolee. Through the opening she saw a time when she would dominate him and he would fulfill her wishes. Having servants had become a thing of the past, but was sorely missed. Perhaps the future held promise for their marriage after all.

Vertiline had the rustic cottage that had been the original Sobearn house cleaned out and outfitted for the married couple. Carolee didn't want to live in the cottage with her husband, but at least they slept separately and she had her own bedroom. She was grateful to Vertiline for suggesting a grace period. By the time he started to think about sexual intercourse, she intended to have him under her thumb, and then *she* would make the decisions about such things.

~~≈✦≈~~

Colonel Marshall was indeed handy around the college, and Carolee could see he enjoyed the work. Mary badgered her husband Frederick to provide supplies from his hardware store at little or no cost to the college. The Colonel put them to good use. He seemed willing to devote his energies to anything that needed maintenance or repair. Among many other tasks, he skillfully replaced rotten fence posts, wielded a scythe to keep the greenery around the campus in its place, and fixed a leak in the roof of the two-story schoolhouse. Since he had some knowledge of carpentry, once the roof leaked no more, he repaired water damage to the ceiling, the wall, and the floor beneath it.

Melancholy and often maudlin, he wasn't a man with whom Carolee wanted to speak. At first, she addressed the Colonel only to ask him to complete tasks around the house and college or to request his participation in an activity requiring a man's strength and ingenuity. With time, requests became demands to complete chores, to relax less and work harder, to keep his mind on his business and nothing more. If he was idle, she invented work for him. Soon he waited on Carolee's every command, fetching for her and performing small tasks with which she could not be bothered.

For the longest time, he seemed content under Carolee's control and she thought nothing about his feelings. If he came too close, she glared at him. When they were alone together, she'd catch him looking at her with a curious longing expression that spoke of a desire she had no inclination to satisfy. Over time she came to hate that look. Whenever she saw it, she'd let out a growl to make sure he kept his distance. They continued to sleep in separate rooms in the rustic cottage and ate their meals with the students in the dining hall.

Saturdays, he ran errands in town and occasionally came home smelling of drink. As long as he did his work, Carolee didn't mind a little drunkenness. The drink did loosened his tongue, though, and exaggerated his mawkish tendencies. Carolee found that growling at him usually shut him up. Once, though, a snarl brought out a flash of anger in his eyes.

"You could treat me to a kind word," he said, his words slightly slurred. "I have given you nothing but respect, and done you no harm."

"You are a pitiful man," Carolee said. "I have nothing for you."

"I have not always been the man you see now. I was heroic during the war. I led a charge to take a Union redoubt." His face contorted with shame and he turned away. "I did not mean to brag," he mumbled. "Please accept my apology."

Carolee walked away without a word.

The Colonel had been at the college for less than six months in the summer of 1881 when, after running errands on a Saturday, he came back stumbling. Carolee didn't like being alone with him in that State. Vertiline had gone to visit a sick patron of the Montcomber Female College. Mary had gone into town to beg Frederick Sneed for a load of gravel to fill holes in the drive that led from the Christiansboro Road to the doors of the school.

Carolee worked on the laundry, taking dried wash from the clothes line into the rustic cottage where the linens for the entire college were stored in an old pantry. She commanded Colonel Marshall to help her fold the sheets and blankets. Over fifty items needed folding, and they got into a rhythm with the task that must have suggested a dance to the Colonel. She'd take up one side of an item, he'd take the other, and they'd match corners and hand them off to one another. He began counting their steps, as if counting a waltz. "One, two, three, four, five, six…one, two, three, four, five, six…" The rhythm helped them progress through the work quickly, but his voice irritated her. She caught his eye and glared at him, yet he continued. With eye contact established, he seemed to think it acceptable to look her in the face. The unpleasant longing expression she hated so much appeared in his features, but also a slight smile.

Carolee frowned, but continued with the folding.

With the next sheet, as Colonel Marshall moved forward to hand off his corners, he swept Carolee into a waltzing embrace. She became immobile, ending the dance.

"Get off me," she said, straining against him.

His eyes changed; the drunken mirth disappeared, replaced by reckless, shameful desire. He gripped her wrists and wrapped his arms around her, pushing her hands behind her back and holding them firmly. His features had a desperate intensity. Carolee cried out, she growled and barked. Since they were inside the thick-walled cottage with the doors and windows shut, it was likely no one could hear them. She struggled against him, pushing with her chest and hips, raising her right knee toward his groin, but found no leverage to deliver a solid blow.

He drove her back against the wall and gripped both her wrists in one of his great hands. With the other he groped for her breasts. His fermented breath added insult to assault as he drove his mouth onto her lips. She tried to bite his face, but he shifted quickly. His mouth moved under her chin, licking and kissing, and then his teeth found her ear and chewed lightly on the lobe. His tongue plunged into the opening. He moaned as she squirmed against him.

"You are my wife," he said, too loud in her ear. "You will obey me for once."

Carolee screamed, but it was cut short as he struck her across the face. He deftly bundled her up and hauled her into his bedroom. Dumping her into his filthy bed, he fell on top of her. She opened her mouth to scream again and he clamped a massive hand over mouth and nose.

Carolee couldn't breathe. She bucked and twisted beneath him, but he rode her, moaning with pleasure. His hand grappled under her skirts and then she felt his fingers inside her.

As she tried to get her teeth into him again, he shifted his hand enough to allow her a breath, but then made sure the passage for air was sealed off again quickly. She clawed at his back, but couldn't penetrate the tough fabric of his shirt. She pulled his hair and he clamped his hand down harder.

Carolee's energy flagged. Her heart was racing and her darkening vision swam sickeningly with pinpricks of light.

He allowed her another breath as he pressed against her, the bulge of his groin becoming larger, his movements more demanding.

If Carolee continued to struggle and became insensible, there was no hope for her. She had to lull him into letting down his guard.

She began to relax by stages. Since struggling against his fingers caused her pain, she relaxed her abdomen first, then her back, legs, arms, and hands. Finally, she allowed her neck and head to become calm.

His fingers inside were warm. She'd pleasured herself often enough to know that she would soon begin to enjoy the sensation. As she moved her hips in response to his probing, she told herself she was giving him what he wanted and biding her time only until he became less vigilant.

Colonel Marshall managed to mount her without relinquishing control. He thrust his penis deep into Carolee and she didn't resist. As his movements became rhythmic, she discovered a depth of sexual pleasure she'd not known before. Her growing desire merged with her fury toward the man. In climax, she imagined her ecstatic physical release as a burst of flame within that burned him out of her and left him writhing in misery and moaning in the throes of death.

But then his sudden writhing and moaning were merely an expression of his own release.

Moments later, an urgent knocking on the cottage door

The miserable creature had had his way.

Again!

Carolee knew that complete denial of the event, involving a full eradication of the memory, could not begin as long as the abomination, Ambrose C. Marshall, existed.

The man must die.

Eventually Mary returned to the college. She'd known of the rape, even as it happened. "I'm sorry I could not help," she said. "If I'd been here, I might have stopped him."

Carolee, hugged her sister, a rare show of affection.

Less than a month earlier, while she and her twin were in town, Carolee dragged Mary with her to view the mummified remains of a bank robber. Students at the college had been talking about the corpse all week. The twins each paid a nickel to see the deceased; a criminal who had been shot and killed while trying to rob the Merchant's Bank of Christiansboro. Since no family had claimed him, he was on display in a stuffy, private parlor in the back of the Harn and Brow Mortuary. The clever mortician, Mr. Werner Wilder, created the display to earn a little extra and promote his skills as an embalmer.

Mr. Wilder, a towheaded man with pink skin, light blue eyes, and pale lashes and brows, led the women into his back parlor to see the bank robber. He appeared to have rarely seen the light of day.

Inside, the air felt close and too warm. The wallpaper had a burgundy flocked pattern that, despite its urn motif, would have been better suited for a brothel. A set of four upholstered chairs sat in a row facing one dark corner.

"The chairs are for those who wish to sit while contemplating the display," Mr. Wilder said.

The dark burden of velvet curtains, with a calla lily pattern in purple on black, had been partly drawn back from a single window to allow scant illumination. Mr. Wilder pulled it back a bit farther to provide additional light to reveal his display.

When Carolee's eyes adjusted to the brighter light, she saw the deceased standing in the corner on a small plinth that might have been part of a monument but for the thin crack running through it.

Mary drew back from the corpse, and Carolee knew the sight brought her sister painful memories of their father.

In his natty blue suit, the dead man almost appeared to be a living presence in the room, despite his stooped posture and the awkward positions of his limbs. His facial features were somewhat crumpled, his nose withered and crooked, but with his eyes closed, he looked to be merely dozing.

"Don't be afraid to touch him," Mr. Wilder said. "He's fully preserved. There's nothing of decay here."

"I don't fear him," Mary said. "He has departed. However, there's something unsettling about his empty husk, standing here as if greeting us. I expect at any moment he might open his mouth and tell us of his suffering in Hell."

"I understand, Mrs. Marshall," Mr. Wilder said.

"I am Mrs. Sneed," Mary said.

"My humblest apologies, Mrs. Sneed," he said, bowing his head briefly. "The two of you look so much alike, and my eyes aren't what they used to be."

"It's quite all right," Mary said.

"As I was saying, I understand. I too feel disquietude when I'm alone with him, but he has not spoken. Don't feel bad—no woman yet has been willing to touch him."

Carolee, sensing a challenge in his words reached out and touched the hand of the corpse.

"Extraordinary, Mrs. Marshall," Mr. Wilder said. "You have the honor of being the first."

"The flesh is solid as a rock," Carolee said.

"Yes, ma'am," the mortician said. "It is the quality of arsenic embalming. The flesh is rendered incorruptible. The law doesn't like it being used because it can hide murder by arsenic poisoning. I fear soon there will be laws passed against its use."

Carolee remembered that conversation when choosing rat poison as a means to dispatch her husband.

Colonel Marshall came home Saturday afternoon drunker than usual. Carolee thought that perhaps he'd become so intoxicated to salve his guilty conscience after what he'd done to her.

She went to the main kitchen in the schoolhouse and loaded a tray with a bowl of rich chicken and barley soup, and a spoon, then took it back to the cottage. Before serving the Colonel, she opened the rat poison canister and stirred some of the paste into the soup broth. He ate all the soup and then lay down on his bed and fell asleep. When he awoke a couple hours later, he began to vomit profusely.

"I'm swearing off liquor," he groaned when he finished, then went back to sleep.

Carolee hoped he had not ejected too much of the poison. Having to dose him a second time would complicate matters.

She rinsed the soup bowl and spoon in the wash basin in her bedroom, then tossed the water into the yard outside the front door of the cottage as she went to join her sisters for an evening playing cards. She noted with satisfaction as she walked across the darkened lawn to the Sobearn house that the quiet evening would give her proud husband the privacy he deserved.

The next day, as she and her sisters sat in the small parlor of the rustic cottage with Dr. Claytor, he noted the Colonel's cause of death on the death certificate as *organ failure due to infection.*

"I was away, playing cards with my sisters." Carolee told him. "Upon my return, I found him vomiting, but he refused assistance when I offered to call on you for help. Despite his distress, I wasn't aware he was in such peril. He went to sleep and I went to bed as well. When I awoke this morning, I found he'd passed away." She was proud of herself for producing the requisite tears. Mary nodded her approval as she sat next to her twin, holding Carolee's pale hands in her own. Vertiline's solemn demeanor persisted throughout the visit, although Carolee was certain the older sister thought only of Colonel Marshall's insurance policy.

Mr. Wilder arrived to take Colonel Marshall away and prepare him for burial. "Good afternoon, Miss Mortlow and Mrs. Sneed," he said with a rather distracted glance at all three. "And my condolences to you, Mrs. Marshall." Again, the pale eyes in his pink face seemed to take in all three women at once. A confused look pinched his features. The sisters were all dressed in black, their mourning clothes nearly identical, and for the first time Carolee realized how much Vertiline favored Mary. Despite Vertiline's additional height, the three must have looked like triplets to Mr. Wilder.

Mary and Vertiline excused themselves, and he seemed somewhat relieved. He turned to the business at hand, but when he saw the condition of the corpse with its blue lips and sunken eyes, he looked at Carolee, suspicion playing about his eyes and mouth. Without another word, however, he fetched his assistant, loaded the body into his wagon, and returned the way he'd come.

Almost a month later, Carolee reluctantly accepted the signs her body had been sending her for some time; she was pregnant. In the spring of 1882, she gave birth to Orphia Sobearn Marshall. Carolee accepted motherhood as part of life, but knew that unlike most parents, her commitment to the wellbeing of her child was largely a charade. At times, the beauty of the infant's large eyes compelled Carolee to hold Orphia close and delight in their shared warmth and life. Then inevitably memories would come of what the bitch had done to her own litter in the garden of Carolee's childhood home. The young mother wondered if she'd do the same as the bitch had done in similar circumstances. Her stomach growling, Carolee would put Orphia down.

The ten-thousand dollar insurance payout upon the death of Colonel Marshall helped to keep the college in business for another fifteen years.

───※───

Recollections trailed away as Carolee of the past joined herself in awareness of the padded cell again.

She reached to feel her twin's reaction to the memories, hoping she'd stimulated a strong response. But Mary remained calm, unfazed by her twin sister's emotional experience. Indeed, she had no sympathy for Carolee at all. Mary had made her feelings clear in the past, as she did presently; that because Carolee always had a choice, she deserved what she'd gotten in life as God's punishment for the sinful decisions she'd made.

"You are a stupid cow," Carolee said aloud. Although she knew her expression did not reach her sister in the form of words, the meaning would be clear. "You accept the concept of free will, but also believe that nothing happens without that God allows it, that all in existence is a product of his plan."

Carolee shook and cried. "How can you have it both ways?"

She watched the random movements of a fly buzzing about her cell, and tried to imagine its haphazard course among the bulges and folds of the canvas padding as something preordained, of having an importance of purpose beyond mere survival.

Impossible, she thought. *It's just looking for food.* She found something beautiful about the creature's mad dash and scramble. Carolee understood it. The insect landed on the padding near her left shoulder. At that moment she loved the fly more than her twin.

"You believe in God so you won't have to think we're alone in the world, without protection. But I am your only protection, Mary, and I'm willing to do whatever is necessary to ensure our survival!"

Abruptly, an impression came to Carolee that Mary wasn't there, wasn't listening. Carolee had felt disconnected from Mary on a few other occasions. Lack of awareness of her sister's experience happened all the time, but not an inability to access it on demand. Carolee suspected that however Mary achieved it, the results were intentional. Mary was keeping secrets, and that was frightening and inequitable.

In frustration, Carolee struck the fly she loved, smashing it against the canvas folds. She pealed its broken body off the wall, and considered it.

"How dare you take advantage of me like that, Mary!" Carolee shouted.

She stuffed the fly in her mouth, ground it to bitter paste, and swallowed.

Chapter 10
Vertiline—Anger

After going over the events surrounding Orphia's death, Mr. Hitchens turned to other discoveries dredged up during the police investigation: those elements of the state's case presented to make Vertiline and her sisters look like cold-hearted criminals. The family's dirty laundry would be aired once again before strangers in the courtroom, but this time, Vertiline hoped Mr. Hitchens would help her take it all down, fold it neatly, and put it away looking much cleaner.

Doing her best to soften her facial features, adopt a less formal posture, and appear open in response to her attorney, Vertiline hoped the jury's impressions of her were improving as she spoke.

"Miss Mortlow," Mr. Hitchens said, "Let's talk about the time before your family moved to New Jersey, when you and your two sisters, the deceased, and her husband all lived in the apartment in Brooklyn."

"Yes, sir."

"Were you surprised to hear that two of your neighbors, a Mrs. Biermann and a Miss Calise, called as witnesses, referred to it as a 'mystery house' and a 'baby farm?'"

"Yes, sir." Vertiline remembered the women well. She considered them troublemakers and busybodies.

Mr. Hitchens consulted his notes at the defense table. "The relevance to this case was not established," he said. "How many children were born to your niece during that time?"

"Orphia had one child shortly after we removed to Brooklyn," Vertiline said evenly, "and another a few years later."

"She gave her first child, a girl named Alberta, up for adoption. Can you tell us why?"

No—the question is too pointed! The dolt wasn't characterizing events to put them in a good light! He'd left that up to her, and she struggled to find the proper words.

"Orphia's husband..." she began haltingly, "had...run away."

Vertiline paused to reflect on her good-for-nothing nephew, Fletcher. She wondered where he'd gone and if he ever found work he was willing to do.

"Is that all?" Mr. Hitchens asked.

"The child..." she began, but her voice trailed off. Vertiline didn't want to admit they had gotten rid of the child merely because Alberta had kept them all up day and night with her crying. Vertiline had not admitted that to herself until the present moment. With the realization, came distress. She glanced quickly at the jury and saw several of the men frown.

"Miss Mortlow?" Mr. Hitchens said.

Vertiline shook off the reverie. "I—I'm sorry." She took a deep breath. "My niece was ill and suffering from severe melancholy. My sisters and I were busy organizing our new business venture, a tutoring service. Orphia neglected the child."

I must appear more caring, and present my decisions as more than merely practical.

"What happened to the second infant—John, was it?"

Again, a blunt question regarding a delicate subject. *Does he have no sense at all?* He made no effort to help her set the scene and create a scenario sympathetic to Vertiline and her sisters. She glared at Mr. Hitchens, then regretted it, knowing the jury saw the expression.

She swallowed hard, relaxed her features, and answered matter-of-factly. "Yes, she named him John. We don't know what happened to him. I was in New Jersey at the time and only know what I was told. Orphia left the apartment one evening while everyone else was occupied with other matters. When she returned, she said she'd lost him, nothing more."

"Objection," Mr. Kalinowski said. "That's hearsay."

Vertiline looked uneasily at the judge. "Sustained," he said.

"What is your understanding about the search for the infant?" Mr. Hitchens asked.

The idiot needed to get off the topic right away! Vertiline ground her teeth and said, "My sisters told me they tried to search for the infant, but had to depend on Orphia to tell them where to look, and she was no help at all."

"Objection," Mr. Kalinowski said. "hearsay."

"Sustained," the judge said. "Miss Mortlow, you will testify only to those things you directly witnessed. You cannot testify about something you did not experience yourself, but that someone told you about."

I must do better. Vertiline felt herself grimacing.

He was just an infant! she thought. *How many of them die every day without help? Orphia wasn't clear-headed. Better to stay quiet about the loss of an infant that had yet to truly live than to destroy the reputation and life of a young woman.*

Vertiline was ashamed of her callous and unreasonable thoughts, but at least she wasn't giving voice to them aloud. Still, the men of the jury watched her doubtfully.

"Your sisters did not notify the authorities," Mr. Hitchens said, "and you didn't notify them either when you found out about it. You don't deny that, do you?"

She would if she could, but Orphia had referred to the infant in the suicide note found with her body. When Vertiline and her sisters were first arrested, they all claimed that Orphia had committed suicide because she was depressed over the loss of her husband and her child, Alberta. The omission of the second child, the infant, John, had raised suspicions. The police investigation went looking for information in Brooklyn at the tenement. They spoke to neighbors, found out about Orphia's second child, and made a search of the tenement.

"No," she said curtly. Vertiline could only hope the jury understood that she was protecting a family member.

"Detective Robert Walker testified that burnt fragments of the bones of a human infant were found in the furnace of the tenement where you and your family lived in Brooklyn. Do you know anything about the tiny bones, Miss Mortlow?"

Although she had her suspicions about Orphia's role, and that of her sister, Carolee, in the disappearance of the infant, thankfully Vertiline didn't *know* the truth.

"No," she said. She clenched her jaw, glanced at the jury, and was disturbed to find she couldn't read their expressions.

"The prosecution's witness, Mrs. Biermann," Mr. Hitchens said, "your neighbor at the tenement in Brooklyn, testified that she started hearing the child's crying around mid-July, and heard the child no more after the end of October. The register of the Bainbridge Hotel in Newark shows that you arrived on July 28th, 1905, which was shortly after your niece, Orphia, gave birth to John. Mrs. Biermann said she saw you coming and going from that dwelling in August, September, and October of that year. Were you present at that abode between the beginning of August 1905 and the end of October of the same year?"

"No, I was not," Vertiline said.

"The Bainbridge Hotel register shows that you left on November 4th, 1905. Is that correct?"

"Yes, sir."

"Do you and your two sisters always wear black?"

What they wore and why was nobody's business, but had to provide some sort of response.

"Yes, we are in mourning for the loss of our father." Vertiline withheld the complete truth.

"And you lost him over forty years ago, during the War Between the States. Is that correct?"

Lost didn't seem like the right word, but would do. "Yes, sir."

"For most, that would seem a long time to be in mourning."

71

"Perhaps."

"Have you and your sisters been misidentified in the past due to the similarity of your clothing and family resemblance?"

"Yes, we are frequently misidentified." When they were all young, the twins succeeded many times in creating a confusion of identity. Their tactic had always been well worth remembering. Vertiline knew from her own experience that those who dealt out punishment had difficulty doing so if they believed an innocent might inadvertently suffer. After they moved to Brooklyn, she insisted that she and her sisters continuously wear mourning clothes.

"Why did you and your sisters move to New Jersey?"

"We purchased a property in East Orange with plans to convert it into a boarding house as a means of creating income to support the family. We intended to all live in the basement apartment of the house and rent the rooms above."

"Thank you, Miss Mortlow," Mr. Hitchens said. "I have no further questions for the witness, Your Honor."

Vertiline couldn't help but smile. Her testimony should help to create reasonable doubt. Mr. Hitchens had done his job. She regretted her total lack of faith in the man. Perhaps he wasn't such a dolt after all.

"Does the prosecution wish to cross-examine the witness?" the judge asked.

"Yes, Your Honor," Mr. Kalinowski said. He stood and approached Vertiline without looking up. He stopped and folded his tiny hands behind his back.

Dread welled up in Vertiline and her heart took a sickening turn in her chest when he lifted his eyes to look at her. She took slow, deep breaths and tried to relax.

"During the investigation, when the detective asked for your opinion as to why Mrs. Orphia Sneed committed suicide," Mr. Kalinowski said, "you said she was sad for the loss of her girl, Alberta, and her husband. Why did you fail to include her infant, John?"

Vertiline glanced down at her hands, gathered herself, and said, "Because she didn't ever care for him."

He paused for a moment, then asked, "Miss Mortlow, why did you move your niece from Brooklyn to East Orange before the house was ready?"

"We thought she would be more comfortable there," Vertiline said, giving a half-truth. "The basement apartment had been finished."

"Not to protect her from an investigation by the Brooklyn police?"

"No...." The jury wouldn't believe her—she could see that. Vertiline wanted to think they were ordinary men, but those eyes—she couldn't help seeing the jury as circling, angry beasts, wanting her blood!

Perhaps if she threw Orphia's bones to the jury, they might concentrate on her and become less interested in Vertiline and her sisters. She would dishonor her niece, but Orphia was gone and largely beyond the need for protection.

"Pardon me," she said, "but I meant to say, 'Yes.' Orphia's melancholy had taken such a toll that she was out of her mind."

The sense of guilt was immediate—Orphia had done nothing to deserve such betrayal. Still, the tactic might achieve the desired results.

"You would have us believe that you knew nothing of the consequences of helping to hide the disappearance of a child, Miss Mortlow?" His sarcasm was thick.

"Yes, sir," Vertiline said, thinking the answer acceptable because he would not be able to prove otherwise.

"You didn't know any better?"

"I suppose that is true," she said, unwilling to give him more.

"Did you do it without a thought in your head?"

Vertiline bristled at the idea that she was thoughtless, but fine…. "Yes, well—"

"Are you saying that a poor, defenseless spinster such as yourself couldn't be expected to know such things, Miss Mortlow?"

"Objection," Mr. Hitchens said. "Your Honor, the prosecution is badgering the witness."

"The objection is overruled," the judge said, his features grave. "I would like to hear the defendant's answer to the question."

Was Mr. Kalinowski arguing that she was stupid and expecting her to agree? He was openly insulting her and the judge allowed it! Vertiline looked to her attorney for a reaction. He returned her gaze, slowly and calmly shaking his head as if he didn't want to be seen doing so. She remembered he was not allowed to communicate with her during cross-examination. He could do nothing more to help!

"Well, I—" Vertiline began, but Mr. Kalinowski interrupted, speaking rapidly.

"Are you saying that despite your much vaunted education in what are merely the simple female concerns of social graces…" Rudely, he turned his back on her and faced the jury as he continued. "…you are merely a person of womanly intelligence, not capable of complex thought and the machinations the state's case suggests?"

"Objection," Mr. Hitchens said more stridently. "The prosecution is badgering the witness, Your Honor!"

"The objection is overruled," the judge said.

Nobody treated Vertiline Mortlow like that! How dare the prosecutor say such things to her without even looking her in the face? How dare the judge tolerate it? Neither of them had any idea what she had survived and what she'd done to preserve and protect her family. And all of the hardship had been brought on by the war crimes of the Union of which they were a part!

"Well, Miss Mortlow?" Mr Kalinowski asked, still not facing her.

Vertiline's outrage boiled over and she stood. "No, sir!" she said too loudly.

"What?" Mr. Kalinowski spun around, looked at her with feigned surprise. "You have a thought in your delicate head?"

"Indeed I *do* have a thought, sir," Vertiline said. She couldn't hide her anger. He was just one of so many who were judging her without knowing anything about her. "I am no *dolt!*" she cried.

Mr. Kalinowski stood with hands on hips, smiling at Vertiline. He was a miserable, small man. *He* was the dolt, with his ill-fitting clothes and his brusque, uncultured manners, like so many of those sitting in the gallery watching her, surprise presently dawning on their dull-witted faces as she finally spoke up for herself. Did they think she would sit and take the abuse forever?

Vertiline saw Mr. Hitchens lean forward with his elbows on the table and rest his chin on his hands. He lifted a finger up to his lips in a covert gesture for her to become silent.

She would do nothing of the kind! "Yes, I protected Orphia from the law," Vertiline said, "and in doing so, I protected my sisters!" She turned to the jury, and looked at them squarely. "Who would not do the same to protect family?" she shouted. "I would do *anything* to protect my sisters!"

Vertiline saw jaws drop, faces wide-eyed with surprise, contempt, and even fear.

The judge's gavel sounded twice, loudly, and all within the courtroom fell silent. "The witness will control herself or she will be removed from the courtroom."

The sober look in the judge's eye brought Vertiline back to herself.

What have I done?

Mr. Hitchens's chagrin was plain to see. As she watched, his expression changed from a grimace to one of sadness.

Still standing, she was dumbstruck by her own actions. Vertiline turned back to the twelve men of the jury. With her outburst, she'd spoiled her one chance to impress them, and in the process had proven the point for the prosecution that she was willing to conspire with her sisters to break the law.

How did he trick me so easily? Surely Mr. Kalinowski was not *that* clever. Something had blunted her cunning—perhaps the poor quality of the food in the jail, which left her weak, or the severe emotional distress.

Suddenly the room didn't have enough air. The underarms of her bodice and sleeves had become darkened with perspiration. The small lunch of beans and bread she'd eaten turned to rocks in her stomach. Glancing at the jury, her anger blossomed, her hatred of them nauseating in its intensity. Harder and darker than ever, their eyes displayed a withering skepticism. As she shrank from their combined gaze, her anger turned inward again.

All was lost if she couldn't pull herself together.

"Your Honor, please ask the witness to take her seat," Mr. Kalinowski said, facing the judge. "I am not finished with my cross-examination."

The prosecutor faced Vertiline with a cold, emotionless face as the judge commanded her to sit. Then Kalinowski turned his back on her again and consulted with an assistant.

Vertiline thought of her daily reminder: *Maintain a sense of personal dignity, for you are useless to your sisters without it.* All she had left was her dignity. That had been all she'd walked away with from the War, nearly fifty years earlier. She couldn't allow the court to take that from her now.

She lowered herself slowly into the hard chair and willed her racing heart to slow. Deep breaths did little to ease Vertiline out of her rage. Tears threatened to spill, but she held them back.

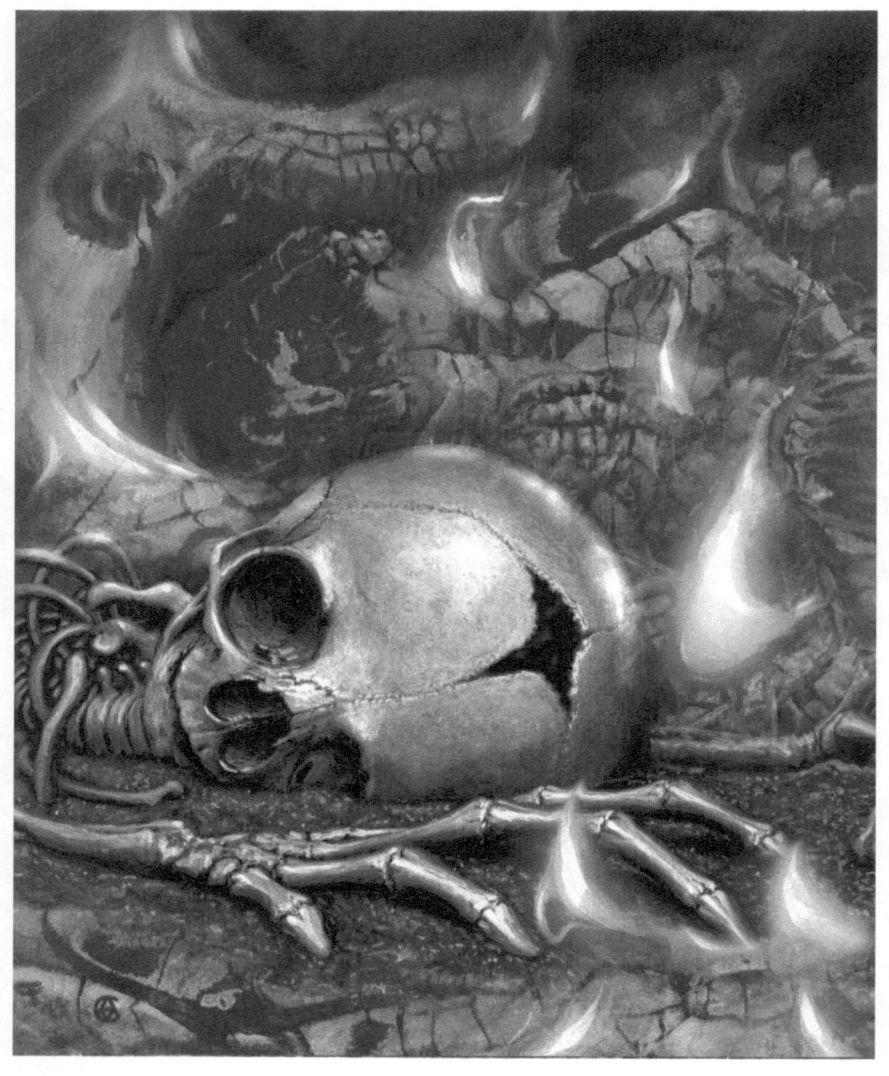

Chapter 11
Vertiline—Childhood's End

Vertiline had never had many friends, but as the year 1861 progressed, social contact of all sorts became less frequent. The young men all left for the fight, and with local leaders urging citizens to do their patriotic duty, women young and old gave most of their time to moral and material support of the war.

In May, Ducy died in her rocking chair. Vertiline found herself mourning the loss more than she had the death of her own mother. Of the two women, when it came to the things that really mattered to a small child, the old black woman had been the superior parent. Ducy had been there to pick the girl up and comfort her when Vertiline was injured physically or emotionally. The old woman had complimented Vertiline for even the smallest graces or achievements. Not that Abigale hadn't tried to do the same when she was available, but the slave governess's advantage had been her nearly constant presence and proximity to Vertiline.

The grief combined with the sudden change in the social environment, left Vertiline lonesome and melancholy. By late summer, she was fed up with loneliness and sorrow. She decided the preposterous war wouldn't go away on its own, and that she must hasten its conclusion by helping her people. Vertiline threw herself into volunteer efforts. She spent most of her spare time for the next two years sewing uniforms and presentation flags for Georgia regiments, and working in kitchens preparing and packaging biscuits, dried vegetables, and bacon for the troops.

Vertiline was sixteen years old in November of 1863, when news came of Union forces breaking through at Chattanooga, Tennessee. Mr. Mortlow gave up his position with the court and stayed home. He spent much time and effort converting a secret room, accessed through a wall panel in his upstairs study, into a hidden larder and hiding place for the family. He directed the household slaves to clear out the numerous short file cabinets, and the dusty stacks of records and documents. Then he personally loaded the room with staples, both dried and canned.

"You're to keep yourself and your sisters close to home," Mr. Mortlow told Vertiline as she looked in on the project in progress.

"But my volunteer work..." Vertiline said. "I am committed to help in the Ratner Kitchen even tonight."

"That must end immediately," Mr. Mortlow said. "Merrill runs errands in town this afternoon—I'll send him by Ratner's to give your regrets." He didn't give her time to respond before changing the subject.

"I can see you know what this room is for, but don't talk about it with anyone, especially the twins. If they ask questions, tell them it's wise to have a place to retreat if there's trouble."

"Yes, Father."

Vertiline's volunteer work for the Confederate cause had begun to give her a sense that she contributed to something important, especially the food preparation, but none of that would matter to Mr. Mortlow. She knew better than to argue with him, and decided she had to be careful not to allow her resentment to show. Nothing would be achieved from angering her father or taking it out on the twins. During the next twelve months, Vertiline's vexation dissipated, but not her disappointment and attendant gloominess.

She visited the hiding place from time to time as the room changed and developed. After having the floor strengthened in one corner, Mr. Mortlow installed a fifty-gallon cistern capable of refilling itself with filtered water from the roof gutters when it rained. The room was a mere crawl space above the front porch, its floor space seven feet by fifteen feet. Although the ceiling was high enough for an adult to stand on one side of the room, it followed the line of the roof, sloping down to the floor on the other side. During the summer the room became unbearably hot, and during the winter months miserably cold and drafty. Her father told her that blocking the vents in the eaves could help regulate the temperature and airflow, but she wasn't reassured. She saw the Sarcophagus, as she called it, as a miserable, cramped cell. Just enough space remained on the floor for four makeshift beds. Having to walk on the bedding to move around upset her.

In early September, 1864, news came of Atlanta burning at the beginning of the Savannah Campaign, later known as Sherman's March to the Sea.

"It's time for you and your sisters to stay home," Mr Mortlow told Vertiline. "All large stores of food have been claimed by the military. The prisoners were released from the penitentiary to help with the coming fight. Many ran off, while others remain in our community. They are desperate, hungry men looking for opportunities. You and your sisters are to remain in the house away from the windows. We don't want anyone outside to be able to see you."

With most of their friends already being kept at home and no chaperone but Mr. Mortlow, who wasn't about to take them anywhere, the girls had become restless.

The twins constantly irritated Vertiline, and their increasing discontent contributed to their tendency to slip into petty bickering. Getting away from them, Vertiline sat at the desk in her father's study to read for a while. In Mr. Mortlow's newspaper, she found an appeal for volunteers to help with wounded soldiers. The work sounded dreadful, but boredom drove her desire to volunteer. Perhaps her father would see that kind of work as important enough to allow her to contribute. She got up and went downstairs.

Asking for permission, Vertiline interrupted a conversation between Mr. Mortlow and Merrill in the kitchen. He turned to her impatiently. "No, you shouldn't see all that, and you and your sisters must be prepared to enter the hiding place at a moment's notice."

He turned back to his servant. "I told you, there isn't enough food for everyone. Use the wagon, take all the servants and go."

"There are bounty hunters, sir," Merrill said, looking away.

Coward, Vertiline thought.

"Yes, they're trying to get rich while they can," Mr. Mortlow said. "You'll have to take your chances. I've written a letter you're to present if you run into trouble. It's the best I can do." He handed an envelope to Merrill.

"Yes, sir," Merrill said, his eyes focused on the oak floorboards. Then he raised his head and looked at Mr. Mortlow as if an idea occurred to him. "I think I may know of a place of safety until the danger passes, if we can get to it."

"Good luck," Mr. Mortlow said, and he shook Merrill's hand.

Vertiline wasn't pleased to see the gesture, but at least the man was leaving. The slaves packed up and left that afternoon with no supplies of any sort.

Because food had become increasingly scarce through the summer, the Mortlows dipped into the stores that had been loaded into their hiding place. With the supplies running low by the first of November, Vertiline noticed that her father was not eating. When she became insistent that he should eat, Mr. Mortlow took her aside.

"I am not eating to make sure there is enough for you and your sisters," he said. "We will not argue about it."

"But Father—" Vertiline began.

The fierce look in his eyes stopped her. "You've heard what I have to say on the matter, young lady. You will not talk about it with your sisters."

Vertiline could only hope their situation improved before her father began to suffer.

"I hate the canned food." Carolee said, as they sat eating in the kitchen. "The tin tastes better than the chicken inside it." She chewed on a piece of lead solder pried off the seam of a can.

"It doesn't matter what you think," Vertiline said. "Spit that out."

Carolee did as she was told, then picked up a biscuit and dropped it onto the table. The food landed with a sharp rap. "I hate these hard things even more."

Mr. Mortlow had long ago given the duty of maintaining discipline for the twins to Vertiline. When he thought they were getting out of hand, he would cut his eyes at Vertiline with a look of exasperation, though lately, he seemed too tired for even that much effort.

Carolee perched on the edge of her chair, elbows on the table, while Mary sat up properly.

"I don't like the dried meat and fruit," Mary said. "Father, you can have mine—I don't want it."

"You could have just a little, Father," Vertiline said.

"I won't argue about it, Vert. You will take care of your sisters and leave me be. Soon, they will like the food well enough."

At first he was miserable and grouchy, but after a time his good humor returned, so Vertiline ceased to worry about him.

On November 21, 1864, as the Union forces drew close, most citizens left Milledgeville, abandoning their homes and allowing slaves to run free.

"You and your sisters are not to leave the house," Mr. Mortlow told Vertiline. "We will all sleep in the hiding place at night from now on."

"Why aren't we going with them?" she asked.

"Because there's nowhere to go and no food out there." He gestured widely.

"I don't want to sleep in the Sarcophagus," Vertiline said quietly, unable to meet her father's eye.

"Don't call it that," he said sternly. "You will do as I say."

"Yes, Father."

Vertiline closed the sheer inner curtains on the front windows of the house to give the family privacy and sat with her sisters to watch the exodus in the street outside. Hundreds of men and women moved steadily southeast along Spring Street, some walking and carrying a few possessions, others riding heavily laden carriages and wagons. The voices coming from those in the street were largely subdued and patient. When someone ran into trouble, others stopped to lend a hand.

Vertiline was relieved to find the twins entertained by the procession. She joined her sisters in making a game of recognizing and pointing out their neighbors as they passed by. The procession also included a variety of animals from fine ponies to draft oxen, and it continued on and off all day in a peaceful fashion.

Mr. Mortlow watched with his daughters for a while. "Not all these folks are from Milledgeville," he said. "Some are from communities to the west of here that have become overrun by Union troops."

By nightfall, when they bedded down in the Sarcophagus, the sounds coming through the porch eaves from the street below had become more disturbing. Although she couldn't understand the voices, Vertiline heard tones of urgency and sometimes anger. Twice she heard shouting and the sounds of a struggle. Vertiline awoke in the night to the sound of gunfire, yelling, and screaming in the distance. Her father awoke as well. He placed a reassuring hand on her shoulder. Vertiline slept fitfully for the rest of the night.

When dawn arrived, Vertiline helped her father secure all the shutters and lock the doors and windows. Then they made hot tea and sat to play cards in Mr. Mortlow's study while the twins continued to sleep.

"Is the enemy in the city?" Vertiline asked fearfully.

"No," he said. "Not yet. Most likely the sounds in the night came from looters and the few folks who remained home defending their property."

Leaning back in his chair and extending his legs under his desk, Mr. Mortlow accidentally kicked something loose. The muzzle of a shot gun slid out from behind the desk, and he got up to retrieve it. He tucked it back into its hiding place and sat back down.

Vertiline gave him a questioning look.

"Just in case," he said.

Her imagination went to work, presenting scenarios in which Yankees broke into the house and her father defended the family with the shotgun.

Mr. Mortlow interrupted her frightful thoughts as he leaned forward and opened the top two drawers of the desk to reveal that each held a revolver. "I want you to know where they are, but think very hard before you try to use one."

He removed the cartridges from one of the pistols and handed it to her. The weight of the thing surprised Vertiline. She held it up and sighted along the barrel. He taught her how to hold it, cock the hammer, and pull the trigger. Then he loaded the cartridges back into the pistol as she watched, and he put it away.

She could not imagine using it properly in an emergency. The thought brought a sting to her eyes and she tasted blood in her mouth, though she wasn't bleeding.

"What we heard last night is only the start of trouble," Mr. Mortlow told Vertiline. "I've decided that starting tonight you girls will stay in the hiding place at all times."

"Father, you are overly cautious," she said. "You would leave us in there while the world goes on around us. If being the woman of the house means I have to keep discipline with my horrid sisters while confined to that dark hole, I don't want it."

His eyes flashed with an astonishing anger and desperation. He grabbed her by the wrist painfully. "You listen to your father, young lady. You have a duty."

They looked at one another for a long moment. Vertiline knew she appeared frightened.

Mr. Mortlow loosened his grip, a troubled look on his face. "I have news from Mr. Shannon." He paused as he did when choosing words carefully.

The Shannon family lived in the house behind the Mortlows'. Ever since the War started, her father and Mr. Shannon had been having conversations through the privet hedge that separated their properties. Lately, they didn't talk much, but Mr. Shannon passed messages along with a newspaper to her father through the hedge every couple of days.

"Mr. Shannon says there are saboteurs and foragers for the Yankees moving through," Mr. Mortlow said to Vertiline. "Bummers, I think he called them. They're looking for food and destroying anything that will help us fight. The militia is trying to keep order, but it's an impossible task." He paused again to let that sink in. "You must keep your sisters happy and quiet. Do you understand how important that is?"

Vertiline had rarely been frightened by her father, but there was such an intensity in his eyes, she turned away. "Yes, Father."

Mr. Mortlow let her go.

As Vertiline moved through the house, gathering up items to load into the Sarcophagus—fresh clothing for everyone, games and books, lamp oil, and an additional chamber pot—she tried to quiet her imagination and not think about what was to come. She and Mr. Mortlow entered the hiding place, and Vertiline woke the twins and told them the news. Mr. Mortlow supported her words with his most stern facial expression, and there was no argument.

Vertiline stuffed rags into the eave vents to keep out the cold, and with time the Sarcophagus became more comfortable. Mr. Mortlow remained in his study most of each day, entering the hiding place only to sleep. They slept in their clothes and washed regularly using rags and a basin.

A more severe rationing of food began. All three girls were hungry and grouchy. Vertiline would hardly know the twins were sixteen years old by their actions. They argued with Vertiline about everything, argued with each other over the pettiest things.

One evening, Mr. Mortlow called Vertiline out of the Sarcophagus to speak to her in private.

"If I hear one more raised voice, I will spank all three of you with my belt." He appeared so tired and thin, she didn't have the heart to argue with him.

"Everyone out there is hungry," he said, with a gesture meant to indicate everything outside the house. "There's nothing to eat. In desperation, *men will do anything.*"

"I understand, Father."

Mr. Mortlow had not spanked her in many years. He was indeed tired if he thought she would fear spanking.

Disciplining the twins seemed an impossible task; Vertiline couldn't make them understand the danger and they would not control themselves.

"You always take the goose track quilt," Carolee complained. "You know it's my favorite and it's the thickest."

"It's not yours," Mary said, "and I need something to soften the hard floorboards."

"You only want it because you know it's my favorite."

"You've already got three quilts. I only have two."

"Mother put red in it for me."

"She put green in it because I asked her to."

"You two will have to share," Vertiline said. "You can stack them all up and sleep side by side."

"No," Carolee said. "I'm mad at her."

"I'm not sleeping near her."

"Then take turns—one gets three quilts one night, the other gets them the next."

"No," Mary said. "If I only get two quilts, I should get the thickest."

Vertiline was about to offer one of her quilts, but Mr. Mortlow had reached the limit of his patience and put an end to the argument. He called Carolee out of the hiding place and took her for a spanking downstairs in the female slave quarters, near the back of the house, where the sound of her crying was muffled. Mary trembled as she stood in the study, waiting her turn. Carolee returned with tears and red-rimmed eyes, but with her mouth pinched tightly shut. The process was repeated with Mary. Mr. Mortlow moved slowly, coming up the stairs behind Mary.

"I can't climb the stairs again," he said, his breath puffing audibly. "Your punishment will take place here in the study. You will not make a sound, Vertiline, or we'll adjourn to the slave quarters and begin again."

The spanking did not bring tears, but a hurt of a different kind, for she'd disappointed her father when he had little strength to spare—he'd clearly worn himself out spanking her sisters.

Thereafter, the twins' arguments flew in whispers that sounded like the fall leaves rustling in the wind as heard through the eave vents. A progressively smaller ration of food over the following week took away much of their remaining energy and spirit, and they became quiet.

⚓

All four were bedded down in the hiding place when Mr. Mortlow gently shook Vertiline awake. He lit a lamp. His trembling hand gently covered her mouth. "A window was broken downstairs," he whispered.

Vertiline was instantly awake, heart pumping too fast.

He put his finger to his lips to signal for silence. "Wake the twins and keep them quiet."

Both the young girls let out a startled moan when roused from sleep. "Intruders in the house," Vertiline whispered.

Mary covered her own mouth.

"Leave me—" Carolee began, but Vertiline put her hand over the girl's mouth.

Carolee panicked and struggled until Vertiline crushed her beneath her body, whispering in her ear, "Someone is in the house. Be quiet."

Carolee became still.

The sounds of doors, cabinets, and drawers being opened came through the walls and floor from downstairs. Soft voices and footsteps shifted below.

Carolee sat silently, her eyes unsettled, mouth open in fear. Mary pulled a quilt up over her head and lay still.

When the sound of footsteps came from the stairs, their father pulled aside a piece of wood he'd hinged over a tiny hole in the wall while preparing the room. Through it, he could look into his study. The hole on the study wall was beneath the base of a framed lithograph print. In the shadow beneath the frame, the small opening could hardly be seen. Loud noises came from downstairs, the crashes of furniture being upset, and a rough and desperate search of the kitchen and pantry. Then footsteps upstairs, getting closer.

Mr. Mortlow reached for Vertiline silently, placing his hand on her shoulder while still maintaining his view through the hole into his study. "Slaves," he whispered. "They're just hungry."

Vertiline heard his desk being searched. The contents of the cabinets in the study were dumped onto the floor. Mr. Mortlow pulled back swiftly from the view hole, startled, and then came the sound of the lithographic print dropping to the floor and the glass in its frame breaking.

The footsteps retreated, but the voices continued in low tones for another hour.

"Go back to sleep," Mr. Mortlow told his daughters, but they all lay awake for some time, listening. Vertiline could not understand the words coming from downstairs.

Finally the twins slept. Vertiline nodded off fitfully several times, but could not remain asleep.

"All is quiet below," her father told her at one point. "I didn't hear them leave. They may have decided to stay the night in the house."

Sometime later, a commotion below suggested the slave were still there. Mr. Mortlow consulted his watch. "It's near dawn," he said. "I think they're leaving before there's light outside."

An hour later he crept out of the hiding place. Before he shut the panel behind him, he said to Vertiline, "If you hear any noises while I'm gone, you stay here with your sisters until long after it's over."

When he was gone, a dread of never seeing him again descended. She sat quietly for an eternity, watching through the hole into the empty study beyond, dimly lit by the early light of the coming day. A deep loneliness settled in, though her sisters breathed softly in sleep not three feet away.

Eventually, Mr. Mortlow returned and opened the panel. "They've gone. I need help covering the window they broke."

Vertiline left the twins sleeping and emerged. The study was a mess, drawers pulled out of the desk, their contents scattered everywhere.

"Father," Vertiline said. "Did they take the extra pistol?"

"They took both—I forgot to bring one with me when I came to bed last night. They found the shotgun and took that as well." His expression mixed fear and regret.

Vertiline felt relieved that the weapons were gone. She wasn't happy with herself for feeling that way, but she had a hard time imagining herself using one of the pistols. She couldn't imagine her father, frail and unsteady as he was from lack of nourishment, would do well with a firearm either.

The state of the study was nothing compared to that of the downstairs. Most of the furniture had been upset, some of it broken, the contents of armoires, cabinets, and shelves strewn about the floors. A delicate Japanese sculptured scene, made of carved pieces of ivory, with a miniature house, trees, a pier, and tiny fisherman, which had always been kept clean and safe under a small, decorative glass-walled box, had been trod upon and crushed on the floor. The item had been a gift to her mother from a friend who had traveled in the East. Vertiline had always marveled at the intricate detail in the carving, and as small as it was, the scene had carried her child's imagination to far off wondrous places. More than ever, childhood seemed far away and lost in time.

She left the carving and the memories where they had fallen, and helped her father right a wardrobe and back the piece of furniture up against the broken window in his bedroom. She could see the shutter had been pried loose outside.

Vertiline started to clean up the mess, but he stopped her. "Leave it. Seen from outside, it will the show that the house has already been looted. Those who see it might move on."

She didn't like it, but understood. Vertiline returned to the hiding place to get some sleep.

∼≺✦≻∼

The sound of explosions joined the gunfire for the next two nights. The Union Army moved through the streets of Milledgeville.

A crashing directly below Vertiline and her sisters startled them, but luckily, no one screamed. Mr. Mortlow hurriedly opened the panel, scrambled awkwardly but quietly into the hiding place, and shut it behind him. Vertiline blew out the lamps that were lit.

Mr. Mortlow peered through the hole in the wall. They heard footsteps.

"Union soldiers," he said. "I see two on the landing, but there might be more downstairs."

The footsteps seemed to make a quick sweep of the house and then they were gone.

"They weren't interested in the house because it has been ransacked," Mr. Mortlow said and he exited the hiding place. Vertiline followed, and they discovered that the front door had been broken off its hinges.

∼≺✦≻∼

The next day, Vertiline was busy keeping her sisters happy with a game of Chinese checkers when her father knocked on the panel that led into the hiding place. She cracked it open and looked out, and he gestured for her to join him in the study. She emerged and shut the panel behind her. With the sky beyond the upstairs windows overcast, she couldn't determine the time of day. The fireplaces had not been lit for weeks, and with the winter weather, the house had become unbearably cold. By contrast, the hiding place, full of quilts and bedding, held their body heat quite well and remained cozy.

Mr. Mortlow sat at his desk in his swivel chair, the one Vertiline and her sisters had dizzied themselves in countless times. He was bundled up in a blanket to stay warm.

"I just spoke with Mr. Shannon in the garden," Mr. Mortlow said. "He says they've destroyed everything, railway lines, telegraph cables, bridges. The Union Army is still here, but he thinks they're in a hurry to move east and that the bummers have done their worst. If we can hold out a little longer..." He paused to peer deeply into Vertiline's frightened eyes. "Can you continue without me? Will you remain hidden until the Union forces have left the area?"

Without him? He would leave the house?

Then Vertiline realized he was talking about death. The date was November 30. He'd been a month without food. He looked so old, his face thin and haggard. His whiskers had grown enough that if trimmed properly he'd have a respectable beard. His hair was long, gray, and disheveled.

"Yes, Father," she said, reaching for him and hugging him tightly. "I promise to protect them."

Horace Mortlow had never been physically affectionate with his daughters, but he returned her embrace with warmth. She could feel his body shaking with the effort.

"I love you, Father," she said, tears in her eyes.

"I love you too, dear Vertiline." He wiped a tear from the corner of her left eye. "Don't cry. You've got to be strong for the twins. Now go to your sisters."

Vertiline didn't want to leave him, but she didn't think he was at death's door quite yet. She nodded her head and retreated back into the Sarcophagus. If she did a better job with her sisters, kept them absolutely quiet, if she troubled her father less, made sure he drank his water and slept regularly, he'd recover his strength.

Mr. Mortlow did not enter the hiding place that night. The next time Vertiline saw him, he was asleep in his swivel chair and would not awaken.

Chapter 12
Mary—Salvation

Mary heard the murmur of voices from others in the building, but couldn't make out what was being said. The sound was calming and she rested comfortably, thinking that her jail cell was a peaceful place to die.

Mary knew she would have to save her twin sister from eternal damnation. Carolee might not have any concern for her immortal soul, but Mary intended that her twin should go with her to Heaven. As their father always said, and Mary's experience bore him out, they were two halves of a whole. She believed that she and her sister would become one and made whole as part of her reward in Heaven.

Carolee was Mary's sinful half, her unbridled emotional self. Much of life would have been terribly dull if not for Carolee's spontaneous emotional outbursts and their consequences, but her animal nature gave her a sense of being separate from Mary when nothing was farther from the truth. Carolee was as wary as a beaten cur and would lash out defensively against what was literally her own flesh and blood. In her recollections, she assigned blame to Mary for events that were part of the greater plan over which no one but the Lord had any control.

Mary knew the difference between sinners punished and sinners rewarded was merely a matter of faith. Since she accepted Jesus as her savior and had faith in the Lord, her twin would join her in Heaven. Carolee really didn't have a choice in the matter, much as Mary had had no choice but to know her sister's delight in taking human life and to receive a certain pleasure from the experience as well.

~~×⚜×~~

Mary's sons, James and Fletcher, were raised primarily at the college because she so rarely went home to her husband, Frederick Sneed. Frederick had finally become fed up with the arrangement, and left Mary and the boys in 1883.

"I'm joining an expedition to explore the Chaco region of Bolivia," he'd told her, trying to make his soft boyish face look proud and brave. He was almost forty years old, but despite his six foot height, he had never looked his age. That appearance of youth and vitality had been a large part of her attraction to him, but as he aged, he'd clearly become self-conscious about his boyish appearance, and affected a deeper tone of voice and a swagger to compensate. The facade was unattractive. "You know Mr. Bauman, the deacon at the church, is enlisting missionaries to help the Bolivian government open up the territory for settlement. I feel the need for adventure before I'm too old. You and I—we spend so little time together, I don't believe I'll be missed. I'll turn the hardware store over to Gerald. I know he'll do his best to represent us. If all goes well, I'll return in the fall in two years."

Frederick then paused to allow Mary to respond. Something about his expression suggested he was providing a test of sorts. She wasn't certain he truly had the courage to go to South America on the adventure, but if he'd hoped she would beg him to stay, he must have been disappointed.

Mary remained silent until he seemed to become somewhat uncomfortable. "Do you have any questions?" he asked.

"No," she said. "I bid you a safe journey."

She felt nothing but relief—he had rarely done more than apologize for his inadequacies.

Within the month, he was gone and she never heard from him again. By 1890, she believed he must surely be dead. Mary lamented only that he'd left no life insurance policy behind from which she and her sisters might benefit. But then proof of his death would have been required to collect, and that was not forthcoming. They never had much to do with one another, and his income from the hardware store didn't keep pace with the slow but steady accumulation of his debt. She was well rid of Frederick, although his brother, Gerald, didn't do much better with the store.

In 1897, the possibility of bankruptcy loomed over the college again. Winifred had kept the school filled with students seemingly with little effort, but Vertiline struggled to do so. Watching Vertiline interact with the students and their parents, Mary realized that until the dementia of her grandmother's later years, Winifred's charming presence at the school had made all the difference.

The sisters sold off most of their grandmother's antique furniture and anything else they thought they could do without. One day, Mary overheard Vertiline speaking to a concerned parent of a student about the look of austerity about the campus. "We keep the school spare to promote a sense of frugality, sobriety, and restraint in the students." The argument seemed to go over well enough. If not the charming presence of Winifred, at least Vertiline was clever.

Carolee's girl, Orphia, was fifteen years old. Willowy and blonde, with fine, pretty features, she was a pleasure for all who met her. She lived in the Sobearn house with her mother and aunts, and trained to be an educator at the college.

Mary's two dark-haired boys, presently in their mid-twenties, had grown into tall, thin young men. James, the older of the two, had deep-set eyes, much like those of his Aunt Vertiline. He had the long Mortlow nose, and a square chin. His hair, with its many licks and whorls, was impossible to tame. Since he didn't bother with it, he always looked rather silly. Mary's younger son had his father's boyish looks, but they were more appropriate at Fletcher's young age, and he seemed to feel no need to compensate with swagger as his father had done.

The two young men had been schooled by their mother and aunts to replace two of the remaining teachers at the college. James taught English, Fletcher mathematics. They lived in the rustic cottage.

Fletcher had been a melancholy child and still slipped into that state easily as an adult. He had always been quite taken with Orphia, ever since her infancy, and was helpful throughout her upbringing. When a boy, he'd played games with her and allowed her to follow him around as he explored the nearby creek and the woods surrounding the campus. When he slipped into a foul mood, she stuck by him. She read aloud to Fletcher from novels such as *The Adventures of Tom Sawyer* and *Uncle Tom's Cabin*, and told him adventure stories of her own creation.

Mary found one tale her niece told inexplicably troubling. She'd walked in on Orphia and Fletcher while they sat on the settee in the parlor of the Sobearn house. They were holding hands, but let go of each other when she entered. After an awkward silence, during which Mary sat down and took up her knitting, Orphia continued her tale.

"Clarence Perforce Tate fell dead with Grandfather's bullet in his heart. When Grandfather tried to walk away, he also fell, his evil opponent's golden bullet in his leg."

Fletcher was captivated as if he'd never heard the tale, and Mary realized she'd never shared the story with her sons. In fact, she hadn't thought of the account for many years.

"Too dangerous to remove," Orphia continued, "it remained in his leg. 'The gold is valuable and well protected,' he told his children. 'If we ever meet with hard times, I'll cut it out and we'll be rich again.'"

Fletcher grinned.

"Who told you that story?" Mary asked.

"It's in Aunt Vertiline's *My Book of Memories*," Orphia said, "that I found was in the attic. Odd that it only has entries from before the War, when she was little."

"Don't ever tell that story again," Mary said. "It's a lie."

Fletcher frowned at his mother.

"Yes, Aunt Mary," Orphia said with a look of hurt. Both she and Fletcher appeared confused. They got up and left the room, looking back over their shoulders as they went.

Mary also found her reaction mysterious and confusing, but the memories the story brought up were too painful to dwell on. Since his death, recollections of her father had always been that way.

Mary was pleased to see the way Orphia could draw Fletcher out. She secretly enjoyed watching them together. If stories failed to make him smile, Orphia resorted to jokes. Mary remembered a charming exchange between the two.

"A gentleman said to his servant, 'Look here, Hester, I found a button from a blouse in my soup.' Hester smiled and said, 'Oh, thank you very much, sir, I've been looking for it everywhere.'"

Fletcher didn't respond to that one at all.

Orphia liked jokes that involved servants. Perhaps she found the concept exotic. She'd heard about the times when the family had slaves before the War. Since then, the family had not been able to afford to have many servants, certainly not ones that would wait on Orphia.

"A lady said to her cook, 'Ann, where did you get the pretty design to mark the edge of the pie crust?' Ann said, 'The teeth, ma'am, I found in the tumbler in your bedroom.'"

That one brought a smile to his face. Orphia was encouraged.

"A maid received a letter saying her mother was sick. She asked her mistress for permission to go home for a few days. 'You may go,' said her mistress, 'only don't be gone longer than necessary. We need you.' A week went by without a word from her. Finally a letter arrived for the mistress. 'Dear ma'am, I will be back soon. Please keep my place. My mother is dying as fast as she can.'"

That one brought guffaws and broke Fletcher from his foul mood.

Orphia learned as many jokes as she could so she would always have a fresh supply whenever Fletcher seemed to need them.

At fifteen Orphia was becoming a young woman. Fletcher doted on her. "She's a delight," he told his mother. "She never has a harsh word for anyone and she has a gift for finding a silver lining in any dark cloud. Orphia can lift me up with a smile. I laugh and enjoy life when she's near."

Mary worried about the nature of the relationship, but her concern was tempered by the fact that Orphia did improve Fletcher's foul moods.

Mary's older son, James, rarely displayed happiness and most often appeared miserable. She watched him with increasing despair. His melancholy had constancy much like that of Colonel Marshall. While the Colonel had merely been defeated, however, the gray cloud within James resulted from deep misgivings about life itself. James stuck close to home and kept his world small. Mary had on occasion wondered if he had received so much teasing about his hair that he trusted no one but his family. He had no friends and no interest in making any. James could turn even the most lighthearted conversation into an exploration of dreadful eventualities. While he professed to enjoy games, his constant scrutiny of his opponents and accusations of cheating turned the form of amusement into misery. He rode his younger brother with worry, pointing out the endless mistakes and unnecessary risks Fletcher took in life.

"I must prevent you from making the mistakes I made," he told Fletcher.

The younger boy gave him a look of skepticism. Certainly the doubt was warranted, for no evidence existed that James ever made mistakes. His failures came frequently, however. Since he'd taken so few risks, he had little experience, and often wasn't successful when attempting something new.

Mary tried to give him a party on his twenty-second birthday, in March of 1897, but he didn't want one. "Give me a life without humankind and I'll be happier," he said. "The world is dangerous enough and will succeed in killing me one day, but it will do so in an honest, straightforward manner. My fellow man would lend me a hand, then use it to take my life."

Mary had often wondered where he learned to be so bombastic. She folded her arms and looked down her nose at him. "That life of yours is a gift from Almighty God," Mary said, putting as much emotion as she could into the statement. "The pleasure and pain of it, like the hot and cold used to temper steel, is meant to strengthen our hearts to withstand eternity in heaven."

James shrugged and turned away.

Almost a year later, Mary found him hopping about in a strange dance as he hung by a rope around his neck from a rafter in the carriage house. He seemed to have chosen the wrong length of rope; enough to allow his feet to barely touch the dirt floor, but not enough to provide the slack he'd need to remove his head from the noose. Mary saw there was nothing within his reach that he could use to help himself out of his predicament. He'd apparently brought an ottoman from the house to stand on, then kicked it out from under himself with enough force that he couldn't retrieved it. The hopping dance was clearly part of his effort to create enough slack in the rope to work the knot loose with his hands.

Mary watched him turn until he caught sight of her. He became still, balanced on the toes of his right foot. A pitiful gurgling sound came from his rope-burned throat and his eyes were creased with shame.

Disgusting and pitiful, Mary thought. Although certain his poor character would not improve while he lived, she had some hope he would be mended in Heaven. Left hanging, he might expire with time, but then someone else might find him before he did so, and she didn't want to suffer the embarrassment. Mary located a sickle and cut him down.

"Pity you did not succeed," she said without inflection.

James turned aside, nodded his head, and slunk away in disgrace.

❦

Mary had not seen Fletcher and Orphia for most of an afternoon in April of 1898. They both had chores to do. Mary went to the cottage and knocked. Fletcher answered the door barefoot, with his shirt buttoned wrong, as if he'd dressed hastily. He reluctantly stepped aside as she pushed her way in.

The interior of the cottage matched his shabby appearance. The boys made little effort to keep the place clean and organized, but they weren't entirely responsible for the state of the interior. The walls and woodwork, nicked and worn over years of various occupants, needed a good coat of paint, and the floor boards needed scrubbing.

"What are you doing?" Mary asked.

"Not a thing, Mother." He stood awkwardly, as if unable to determine his next move.

"You must be doing something," she said, moving toward the bedroom door. "No one ever does nothing. Why haven't you swept the classrooms and emptied the rubbish bins?"

Fletcher tried to stay between her and the bedroom door.

"Have you seen Orphia? She has work to do, too."

A telltale look appeared on his face when he heard his cousin's name. Mary tried to go around him to the bedroom door.

He stood in her way again. "Please, Mother, don't."

"Don't what?" Mary asked, but she already knew. She brushed past him and looked into the bedroom. Orphia sat up in the bed, the bedclothes gathered around her.

Mary turned to Fletcher. "You will make her whole again with marriage."

"Yes, Mother, gladly."

She could see he wanted to smile, but her scowl wouldn't allow it.

"Orphia," she said, calling through the door.

"Yes, Aunt Mary?"

"Dress yourself and do your chores."

Mary waited to smile until she had left the cottage.

Mary told her sisters about the compromising position in which she'd caught Fletcher and Orphia, and about James's attempted suicide. Carolee seemed uninterested in the news about James. Concerning her daughter's involvement with Fletcher, Mary had reasoned the advantages out for Carolee—the more insular the family was in their relationships, the more easily their secrets could be kept. Carolee agreed with her. Vertiline was clearly more interested in the news about Mary's son, James.

In May, 1898, after Orphia and Fletcher's wedding at the Baptist Church of Christiansboro, the nuptial celebration continued with a picnic on the lawn of the college campus for the family, the three non-family teachers of the college, and the minister who presided over the wedding.

The warm spring day was a fresh and beautiful relief after a long dull winter. The promise of life's renewal surrounded them; flowers blooming on the campus, young green leaves filling out the trees, and the sun shining brightly in a blue sky.

Sandwiches were served at the picnic. Then came the wedding cake, a small chocolate confection served with homemade ice cream. Mary was disgusted to see the frozen portion of the treat came out a bit soft because James got a late start on cranking the ice cream churn and had done so in an unenthusiastic manner that included several breaks.

After most of the guests departed, while the young adults played horseshoes, Vertiline leaned toward Mary and whispered, "I took out a life insurance policy on James."

The older sister had always been the highest authority since their father died, but in Mary's role as bookkeeper, she considered Vertiline's willingness to take the action without consultation as an affront. "You know we can't afford such a thing."

"You cheated," James shouted.

"How does one cheat at horseshoes?" Fletcher asked as the contestants moved to the farther stake to continue the game. "I was behind the line."

James remained quarrelsome, but as he moved farther away, at least his words became indistinct.

Vertiline glanced in his direction then back at Mary, an exasperated look on her face. "We can if it pays off soon."

Mary could only raise an eyebrow as she thought of the implication of Vertiline's statement.

"You must persuade him to do it properly," Vertiline said, "so it will appear as an accident."

None of the sisters liked James, but Mary had to claim him as her own, a position that grew more intolerable by the day. Yes, she could formulate an argument that he would take to heart. Even as the matter was considered, God provided inspiration. The act would take courage on James's part. That in itself was worrisome.

"You scolded me for wanting to throw away God's *gift*." James's face twisted in consternation.

"I did," Mary said, "but—"

"I believe I purposely made the rope too long," he said. "I'm afraid I'll be damned to hell if I succeed."

"Yes, I scolded," she said, "but that was before I saw God's purpose for you. You attend church regularly. You are not a lost sinner. While suicide is a sin, forgiveness is guaranteed because you have been baptized and are born again in the faith of Jesus Christ, our Lord."

Mary smiled and stroked James's forehead, thinking of him as a small child afraid of the dark.

"You have been miserable in life," she said. "Life is unfair and too difficult for a man with your sensibilities. Decisions have always weighed heavily upon your heart. Trust me to make the decision for you. I don't make it lightly. As I've explained, your family and the college will benefit greatly."

"Would you miss me?" he asked, pitifully.

"Of course I will." Mary scolded herself silently for the lie.

She launched into a retelling of her father's sacrifice during the War Between the States, then concluding with, "And your heroic sacrifice, just like your grandfather's, will live in our hearts forever."

For reasons unclear to her, she found using her father's role during the war as an example troublesome and frustrating. Her words failed to express the power of the family's experience during that period. Mary knew a greater, more inspiring truth existed, but whatever was missing from her tale, the substance of it eluded her. Perhaps that was for the best, however, because for reasons equally unclear to her, she knew that James could not—or should not—be told.

"Yes, I always enjoyed hearing about him." James produced a weak smile. "I've never felt as though I had much to contribute to the family. That's a part of my sadness." His smile became larger. "Perhaps I've finally found what I have to offer."

Late fall of 1898, James boarded a train headed for Louisville, Kentucky, with the intention of leaping from the locomotive while it moved at great speed, and dashing his brains out on the rough ballast around the tracks. He leapt shortly after the train left the station in Christiansboro, before much speed had accumulated. He broke a leg in the fall and was a burden to the family until he healed many months later.

Spring of 1900, James leapt into a well, but he thrashed about and cried so long and hard for help that trying to ignore him became an embarrassment, and a rescue commenced. With each attempt on his life, the activity and drama served only to draw unwanted attention from the parents of the college students and from folks in town.

"We cannot withstand the scrutiny," Vertiline told her sisters. "We must put an end to it or journalists from the Christiansboro Democrat will come out here and meddle in our business."

"I'll have a talk with James," Mary said.

Years would pass before Mary had the full story of what happened next. Carolee obviously tried to conceal the truth by not thinking about it, but piece by piece Mary experienced her sister's recollections until the puzzle was complete.

When Carolee heard Vertiline say, "put an end to it," she'd taken a different meaning from the words. The next afternoon, Carolee called on James to meet her in the carriage house to help her with a sticky brake lever on the buckboard. In preparation for their meeting, she took a damp mop, a pie tin, a box of matches, and a cigar of James's favorite brand with her. Once in the carriage house, she opened both of the large double doors. She leaned the mop against a wall, then opened a can of kerosene, poured some in a small bucket and some in her pie tin, and set them down by the door. Carolee cleared everything, including saw dust and straw, from a broad section of the dirt floor inside the structure. She set the cigar and the box of matches in the center of the area, and placed several empty kerosene lamps on the floor nearby. Picking up her pie tin filled with kerosene, she hid behind one of the large double-doors and waited.

When James arrived, he bent over to pick up the cigar and match box. He looked at the label on the cigar and smiled. As Carolee had hoped, he put the smelly brown cylinder of tobacco in his mouth, then took a match from the box to light it. While James stood rolling the cigar in the match flame to get it evenly lit, Carolee stepped out from behind the door and doused his upper torso with the fuel. The kerosene splashed up off his chest and the fumes ignited. His face and torso went up in flames. James cried out, turning. Carolee picked up the small bucket and tossed its fuel onto his back and lower torso. As the flames raced down his body, engulfing him entirely, she got behind him with the damp mop and used the implement to shove him out of the carriage house. Reeling, he ran out onto the campus lawn. He screamed once clearly, but his second effort sounded more like gargling. Finally, James fell to the ground and died in a gurgling, writhing, blackening heap.

The kerosene that hit the dirt floor in the carriage house had ignited and burned out quickly, without setting the structure ablaze. Carolee dropped the small bucket and mop. She set the open can of kerosene on the floor lying on its side and allowed the majority of its contents to spill and soak into the dirt. Taking up her pie tin and mop, she exited through the small add-on shed attached to the rear of the carriage house, dashed through the copse of trees that stood between it and the Sobearn house, and entered through the kitchen door. Apparently no one saw her. She washed the pie tin and mop, then the sink, and hurried out to the lawn where she tried to appear surprised by all the commotion.

That evening, as the sisters sat in the parlor of the Sobearn House after a light supper, Mary, still ignorant of the facts, tried to discuss with Vertiline and Carolee what had happened.

"James didn't have the courage to—" she began, but Carolee interrupted.

"I can explain what happened."

"No," Vertiline cut her off, her voice too loud and shrill. What happened had obviously shaken her. "I don't want to know anything about what you two did today." Apparently, that was the end of the matter. Nothing more was said.

The insurance company threatened an investigation, but although the manner of James's death was extraordinary, as far as local law enforcement was concerned, the women of the Montcomber Female College were above reproach. Common wisdom held that the accident-prone man—everyone in the community knew by then that he'd fallen from a train and nearly drowned in a well—set himself ablaze while smoking and filling lamps in the carriage house.

Eventually the insurance company paid the twelve thousand dollar claim.

⟳❧⟳

On a Monday shortly after the funeral of James Sneed, Mr. Wilder of Harn and Brow Mortuary approached Mary on Main Street in Christiansboro while she was on her way to the bank. She stopped to speak with him. He gave no greeting, but launched into something that seemed rehearsed. "I am well aware of the method by which your husband was murdered," he said.

The words startled Mary. Had her husband been found?

"I remember telling you and your sister about arsenic embalming," he continued, his pale eyes narrowed sharply as if he could use them to pin Mary to where she stood. "My suspicions were raised when Colonel Marshall died shortly thereafter. I took samples of his tissues before I embalmed him, tested them, and found just what I expected."

What he said wasn't about Frederick at all. He thought he spoke to Carolee! Dressed in mourning clothes the sisters looked much alike. He thought he knew something about what her twin had done. Mary was familiar with taking blame for Carolee's actions, and knew how to use the confusion of identity to throw off suspicion. She donned an expression of intense concern.

"I've thought about this for a long time," he said. "With the suspicious death of another man in your family, I know you're up to no good."

Mary coaxed tears and allowed them to spill down her cheeks.

Mr. Wilder appeared somewhat unnerved by the emotional display, but he plunged forward, speaking rapidly as if he knew his time on stage must soon end. "For my continued silence in the matter, I'd like an occasional visit by your female students. After the circus came to town last summer I expanded my display of the embalmed to include stillborn Siamese twins and a baby elephant. You will recruit those students interested in a private viewing of these curiosities and bring them one at a time to my establishment to be left there over night. I have an anesthetic to use so that they will not be aware of what transpires and will lack memory of it. I'll return them to the school before dawn the next day, so they can be placed in their beds while still asleep. You will organize these rendezvous and work out the details secretly with me or I'll go to the law."

He looked at her expectantly, with an expression that urged her to respond quickly. He pulled at the collar at his plump, pink neck and licked his dry red lips. His disgusting and depraved intentions toward the girls of the college did not bear thinking about. The plan seemed poorly conceived, but that didn't change the fact that he'd made a significant threat.

"But sir," she said, her voice cracking with feigned distress, "I'm Mary."

Mr. Wilder's eyes grew large and his mouth opened, but nothing emerged. He stood staring at her.

"I don't know what you mean," Mary said. "The loss of my son was a terrible accident."

Mr. Wilder backed away, and finally his mouth began to work again. "I'm sorry, Mrs. Sneed." One of his soft, little hands went to his forehead. "A—a terrible joke. Something I ate has left me—please, excuse me." He hurried away.

Although she'd gotten the upper hand, Mary finished her errands in a troubled state.

That afternoon, when she returned home, she told her sisters about the conversation while they stood in the kitchen of the Sobearn House.

"I will take care of it!" Carolee said, a murderous look in her eye.

"No," Vertiline said. "He believes he's revealed himself to the wrong party. It may well be he'll let it drop for fear that his wicked desires will be exposed to the community." She paused and then took Carolee by the shoulders. "Did you poison your husband?"

Mary watched Carolee's jaw muscles clench, and her eyes turn away from her older sister.

"Did you poison your husband?" Vertiline asked again, her tone demanding, but incredulous and disgusted.

Still unwilling or unable to look at her older sister, Carolee wouldn't answer. After a time, Vertiline released her. "Get out of my sight," she said. She covered her mouth with a hand and sat down heavily at the table as Carolee left the kitchen.

Throughout the rest of the day, whenever Mary saw her twin, Carolee appeared restless and testy, her thoughts far removed from whatever she was doing. She didn't turn up for the evening meal.

Mary knew Carolee had gone to town after dark with a can of kerosene. Mary didn't tell Vertiline because she would have tried to stop Carolee, and the evil man needed to burn.

⚓

News came to the college the next day that the Harn and Brow Mortuary had gone up in flames, taking with it two other establishments in downtown Christiansboro. Mr. Wilder survived the blaze.

The older sister called a meeting with the twins in the kitchen of the Sobearn house. Once they had assembled, Vertiline seemed unable to look at Carolee. The three sat silently at the kitchen table for a moment as Vertiline stared mutely at the freshly scrubbed tabletop. "Soon we'll reach the semester break," she said finally. "We must close our accounts at the bank, pack up, and leave."

"But we have taken tuition for next semester," Mary said.

"He won't do anything after what I've done," Carolee said quietly. "He'll be too afraid of us."

"*Us!*" Vertiline bore down on Carolee with her eyes. "You talk of *us*, but don't consult *us* before wreaking havoc. You'll be our ruin. We would do well to turn you over to the law, but you are our sister. You *are* one of *us!*"

99

Mary watched Carolee cringe at the implied volume in Vertiline's voice. Although the older sister's words came out barely above a whisper, they seemed to thunder in Mary's head.

"He was a danger in the community," Carolee said, her voice truly a whisper.

"*As are you,*" Vertiline said slowly. "You don't know the man, what he might do. You have opened our lives up to possible calamity. We can't remain here to find out what might happen."

Carolee seemed unwilling to challenge Vertiline further, but she obviously wasn't happy.

"What of the tuition?" Mary asked.

"We'll return it with our regrets. If we leave Virginia, no one will come after us."

Mary wasn't frightened of what the future might hold. She looked forward to the change in their lives.

⸎

Mary, Carolee, Vertiline, Fletcher, and Orphia packed up and left the college the next day without telling the few remaining staff of their plans. They traveled from Christiansboro by train with few belongings to New York. Mary had told Fletcher that the college failed financially and the family chose to move to Brooklyn because of the opportunities the city offered.

Mary watched her son on the train. Fletcher was down in the mouth about the move.

Orphia seemed to have noticed his foul mood as well. "I'm ready for a great adventure," she told him. "That's what it will be for the both of us, I'm certain. We'll start our family in one of the greatest cities in the world, where anything is possible. Our future will be bright."

Fletcher's attempt at a smile looked more like a scowl.

"Here's a joke that takes place in New York," Orphia said, smiling. "Fletcher Sneed bumps into a policeman directing traffic on a Brooklyn street."

Fletcher's smile become more genuine as she continued.

"'Look here, confound you!' says the policeman, 'I won't have this. Do you think I'm a fool?'"

Her eyes sparkled with mischief. "'Sorry, sir,' Fletcher says, 'I can't say for certain. I only came here yesterday from Virginia.'"

Fletcher's lips twisted in an effort not to smile. Orphia snickered at him and he let go with a great belly laugh.

If not for Orphia, Mary thought, *Fletcher too might be an embarrass-*

ment.

The family settled into a second floor apartment in a tenement on Bedford Avenue in the Eastern District of Brooklyn in late summer of 1900.

~~✤~~

Yes, Mary thought, *Carolee created most of the trouble in our lives. Even if she were a separate being, she couldn't reasonably blame me for the pain in her life.*

I am not completely innocent. Mary thought about what happened to Orphia's infant. *I will have to answer for that.*

Mary allowed a cockroach to crawl on her without lifting a hand against it. As she lay on her back in the jail cell, her head turned to her left, she watched the creature walk along her forearm. She couldn't feel its movement. If she wasn't looking at the insect, she wouldn't know it was there.

Mary noticed how quiet the jail had become. Was it possible all the prisoners had become occupied with silent activities, or was her hearing failing? As her peripheral vision darkened, she got the impression that she saw the insect at a great distance through a telescope. The effect was momentarily interesting, but then she realized with a burst of panic that it occurred along with the silence because her faculties were deteriorating from lack of sustenance. Her heart beat rapidly for a moment, then slowed again as she willed herself to relax and let go.

Mary thought of her son, James. She would see him again soon. She had not missed him. He had been so miserable in life that those around him had become miserable as well. Made whole in Heaven, he would be a pleasure.

She would see her father and her mother—only vague recollections of Abigale existed—and, of course, she would see Orphia's sweet infant, John. Imagination pictured him as a plump, pink baby in Heaven, but that raised the question of whether he'd grow over the course of eternity.

Seeing them all might have to wait, however; Mary would not enter Heaven without Carolee. Her sister was so obstinate, she might rather suffer the flames of Hell than admit the existence of God. She imagined Carolee thumbing her nose at Jehovah as he sat in judgment.

Mary would wait at the gates of Heaven for her twin and drag her in if necessary.

Chapter 13
Vertiline—Bargaining

The prosecutor's consultation with his assistant lasted long enough that Vertiline had gotten a grip on herself. Sitting in the witness chair, waiting for him to resume his cross-examination, she considered praying, something she hadn't done since childhood. Although Vertiline had kept an outward appearance of piety, she had abandoned God and religion long ago. Nevertheless, desperation drove her to bowed her head and try for help, her lips moving silently in prayer. "Please, Lord, help me. Help Carolee and Mary. If the court were to find us blameless, for the rest of my life, I'll..." What? What did she have to offer? Currently she and her sisters had little but debt. Her prospects were grim. "...I'll spread your message and give all I can to the Baptist Church." The offer didn't seem like much, and surely God would know she'd rarely given anything to charity in the past. She wasn't likely to have much in the future.

What outcome was desirable beyond acquittal? Life had not been good for a long time. Maintaining a protective distance from everyone, she had made no friends, but at least she'd had the respect of others for most of her life. She would never have that respect again, even if acquitted, but instead would suffer an ignominious fate much like that of Lizzie Borden.

Still, Vertiline was willing, and perhaps the Lord would see that.

The prosecuting attorney had so far prepared all the lumber for her coffin. Finished with his consultation at present, Mr. Kalinowski provided nails of sharp, sarcastic language, and penetrating stares to hammer it all together.

"Although your niece was found dead in your basement apartment, Miss Mortlow, a suicide note discovered nearby, the police report, as we've heard, states that there were no writing implements or ink to be found on the premises. How do you think your niece managed that?"

Mr. Kalinowski excelled at making the circumstances sound ghastly.

"I don't know. I wasn't there," she said flatly, trying not to respond to his sarcastic tone.

"Your niece must have been clever indeed."

"Perhaps one of my sisters removed the writing materials when they went for the doctor."

"That's speculation, Miss Mortlow," he said.

"Did you ask them if they had done so?" she asked.

"Your Honor, please instruct the witness to confine herself to answering the questions."

"The witness will provide only answers," the judge said. "The prosecution will refrain from making comments about the deceased's character."

"Yes, Your Honor," the prosecutor said.

Vertiline silently begged for some sign that her prayer was heard. She needed something to give her hope. At the very least, God could give her some physical relief.

Her silk and taffeta mourning garments were plastered to her with perspiration. Her hips and back ached. She'd visited the lavatory before questioning began, but needed to do so again. A nervous cough put pressure on her bladder, and she felt the dampness in her diaper increasing. All she had left in the world was her pride. Yet more than ever, dignity had become merely a matter of appearance. She dreaded the possibility that the diaper might become so overburdened with liquid that it would leak and others might see a dark stain on her skirt when she stood to leave the witness stand.

If her sisters weren't part of her consideration, and Vertiline was given the choice between continuing the cross-examination and immediate execution for the murder of Orphia, she might choose the latter.

"Around the time of Mrs. Orphia Sneed's death," Mr. Kalinowski said, "were you spending time at the 3550 Barns Street address, as was noted by several of your neighbors?"

The roof and walls of the house had been repaired. With the dampness gone from the basement, the space was converted into living quarters with running water for a bathroom and kitchen, and a stove for heating and cooking. The basement apartment, the size of the footprint of the house, would eventually shelter all three sisters, but currently supplies for work on the interior upstairs occupied much of the floor space.

"No, sir," Vertiline said. "I was staying at the Bainbridge hotel, because there wasn't enough room yet in the basement apartment."

"Since Mrs. Carolee Marshall had been sharing the room with you at the hotel, didn't you wonder what had become of her, why she didn't return the night of her arrest, after your sisters were taken into custody?"

"I wasn't overly concerned until a couple of days later," Vertiline lied.

"Although Mrs. Marshall sent a message to you at the Bainbridge Hotel after her arrest, isn't it true that you made no effort to communicate with your sisters in the three days that followed?"

"That's correct." Carolee's message told of Orphia's death, the twins' arrest, and the police investigation. Vertiline had spent those days fretting over what to do, not eating or sleeping, unable to decide whether to try to help her sisters or flee.

"For three days, we knocked on your door, trying to speak to you, isn't that right, Miss Mortlow?"

"Yes, sir." There was no point denying knowledge of it. Vertiline could characterize events to make herself look better to the jury, but Mr. Kalinowski's questions gave her no room to do so. If she tried, he'd have the judge silence her again with another admonishment.

She willed the stenographer to record the testimony differently, to embellish her answers with words she could not speak, but even if she succeeded in magically altering the record, the jury heard only what she said.

Mr. Hitchens showed little interest in the questioning. Again, he seemed unwilling to challenge his opponent's assumptions. Her positive feelings about Mr. Hitchens's direct examination of her had evaporated. He sat at the defense table with his legs spread wide. Food stains marred the front of his coat while perspiration darkened the fabric under his arms. Even if he were interested in presenting a strong defense, why would anyone respect him enough to listen?

"Finally," Mr. Kalinowski said, "the police got the key to your room from the hotel manager, opened your door, and took you to the station for questioning. Isn't that right?"

"Yes, sir." Vertiline looked down, feeling again the terror of that afternoon, when the police barged into her room and escorted her through the lobby of the hotel, while the flashes of photographers tried to catch the moment of her humiliation.

"What was your explanation to investigators for not wanting to talk to the police for those three days, Miss Mortlow?"

"I didn't want to have to talk to the members of the press who were following the investigators." Of course that was only a small part of the truth.

"Since you didn't leave the room, and therefore didn't know about the press's interest in the case until afterward, that was a rather convenient response on your part, wasn't it, Miss Mortlow?"

"No, sir," Vertiline said. She sensed that he wanted a further explanation, but she wouldn't give it to him.

"You knew the police wanted to talk to you about the death of your niece, didn't you?"

"Yes, I knew they wanted to talk about Orphia's suicide."

"That's your characterization, Miss Mortlow," he said. "When you emerged from your hotel room, you were taken into custody and later charged with murder. Isn't that right?"

"Yes, sir."

Mr. Kalinowski lifted from the prosecution table a dark leather-bound object Vertiline recognized as a trifold correspondence folio given to her for Christmas one year by her Grandmother, Winifred Sobearn. "Is this your folio, referred to in earlier testimony?"

"Yes, sir." Despite knowing her restless movements promoted the idea that she was guilty, Vertiline shifted in her seat, trying to relieve the ache in her hips and back and give her bladder more room.

Mr Kalinowski handed the folio to Vertiline and she took it, glad for something to look at as a distraction from her discomfort. After the police had finished their search of the 3550 Barns Street house, a member of the press broke into the basement apartment and found the folio in a cabinet in her bedroom. The reporter's name was Howard Strauss, and he worked for the Jersey Star Journal. To Vertiline, he was a low-life criminal who had burglarized her home. Worse, the police knew about it, but had not charged him with the crime.

"Would you please remind us what was found inside the folio, Miss Mortlow?"

He tried to make eye contact with her, but she wouldn't allow that to happen. When Vertiline failed to answer his question, the prosecutor answered for her. "It held a suicide note for every occasion, didn't it Miss Mortlow?

"The prosecution will allow the witness to answer the questions," the judge said.

"Yes, Your Honor."

"It held several different suicide notes," Vertiline said. She opened the folio and thumbed through it idly. The investigators had removed the notes from the folio and saved them separately as evidence. Mary had stored the suicide notes in the folio without Vertiline's knowledge, no doubt never dreaming the police would take such an interest in Orphia's death that they would search the apartment.

"Although our handwriting expert says you wrote the notes, you still claim that Mrs. Orphia Sneed wrote them, isn't that correct Miss Mortlow?"

"Yes, sir." Vertiline tried to lean back a little. A muscle spasmed in her lower back, and she sat up again, grimacing.

"If what you say is true, can you explain why you would have among your effects suicide notes of such variety written by the deceased?" Mr Kalinowski spoke too loudly, while presenting an ironical smile to his audience; the jury and the gawking members of the public in the gallery. He was a politician, an actor, or worse—a physician selling a new cure.

Her physical misery beginning to overshadow the injury of the man's insults, Vertiline thought that in another circumstance, he might have been laughable. She struggled to hold herself together and speak to him without stumbling.

"As you may know, those of refined bearing and education are in the habit of revealing their thoughts and motivations upon taking momentous action," Vertiline began.

Mr. Kalinowski smiled broadly. That he enjoyed hearing what she had to say told her that he thought she did his job for him. Otherwise he would not have allowed her to engage in such explanation. She knew her words sounded like self-justifying and the jury didn't appear receptive, but she had to go on.

"My dear niece, Orphia was merely looking for the best way to express what was in her heart, creating several drafts until she was satisfied with the language. In her long suffering she contemplated the terrible choice many times. Each time we found a note, we took it away to discourage her."

Stifled laughter and murmurs of astonishment rose up from the public gallery, and Kalinowski's smile became larger. The judge leaned forward, took up his gavel and tapped it once, sharply. "Silence or I'll have you put out," he said to the gallery.

With brows raised and mouth open in a look of mock-innocence, Mr. Kalinowski spread his arms, palms upward, and made a slow circle as he took in the jury and gallery. "Come now, Miss Mortlow," he said in a patronizing tone, "the handwriting is identical to your own."

"Orphia was my student," Vertiline said, "a very good student. As an educator of social graces to young women, my instruction in penmanship is more precise than the Palmer Method, requiring a rigid adherence to a specific ideal standard of cursive structure. This is truly the only way to ensure that all who read can understand what is written by all who write."

Although Orphia's suicide notes were removed from the folio, several pieces of Vertiline's correspondence remained, as well as numerous folded pages in a pocket in the back cover. Looking for more distraction from her physical distress, she straightened the dogeared corners of the pages and wondered what they were. Then she recognized them as essays by her students. Over her years of teaching she'd asked her favorite students if she could keep some of their best work as mementos. Most students were happy to allow the request, and she stored the essays she collected in the back of the folio. Vertiline wished she could read some of the excellent prose instead of having to endure the drama in the courtroom.

"All my students have the distinctive, yet conservative handwriting style developed from my method," she continued, taking shallow breaths. "My niece's handwriting was impeccably proper and naturally identical to my own, just as mine is identical to that of my teacher, my grandmother, Winifred Sobearn."

"Miss Mortlow, that is merely a self-serving statement." Mr. Kalinowski's smirk said that he had Vertiline right where he wanted her.

"We have no documents that we know to a certainty are written by your niece, even those that appear to bear her signature. Our handwriting expert, Mr. Beaumont, says they all belong to you."

"Mr. Beaumont would then have to say the same of all my students' work," she said, thinking about the essays again. Then she realized that the prosecution had never said anything about them. If they had inspected the essays, they might have merely glanced at them quickly, assumed they were Vertiline's writing as well, and put them back where they found them.

She pulled the folded pieces of paper from the back of the folio and offered them to Mr. Kalinowski. As she leaned forward, she grimaced with pain, but composed herself and said in a strained voice, "Did you have Mr. Beaumont look through their work? These essays are all written by different students, but you'll find the handwriting is the same."

Mr Kalinowski's eyes narrowed. His features moving toward concern, he took the pages, opened them one at a time. He looked at her attorney.

Vertiline saw Mr. Hitchens shrug.

Nobody thought to look at the essays! I, too, had forgotten about them.

"For all we know you wrote these yourself," Mr. Kalinowski said.

"Each essay is written with a different pen or pencil. The ink is not the same for all of them. Do you see the names at the top of each page? I'm certain you could locate several of these fine women to testify."

As Mr. Kalinowski continued looking through the pages, his lips were pinched tightly together. Vertiline felt her bladder let go a little, leaking into her diaper, but the prosecutor's expression kept her spellbound.

He's worried!

The prosecutor looked at her attorney again. Mr. Hitchens raised his eyebrows and tilted his head questioningly.

After a moment, Mr. Kalinowski turned to the judge. "Your Honor, may we have a recess? The prosecution needs to speak with council."

Could this be a sign that God had come to her aid? Vertiline could feel hope blossoming in her heart, and that took away some of the pain in her joints.

"Very well," the Judge said. "The court is in recess until Friday at noon."

Vertiline was so startled when the judge struck the sound block with his gavel, her bladder let go. With what had just happened, that was the least of her concern.

Chapter 14
Vertiline—Reflection

Upon leaving the courtroom, Vertiline was taken under guard to a lavatory in the Tombs where she washed and changed into her jailhouse shift. She was then placed in one of the meeting rooms, also part of the Tombs, for what purpose she didn't know. Sitting in a hard chair, she leaned on the table with her elbows, against all her training.

After her initial excitement over the prosecution's reaction to the essays, she feared that Mr. Kalinowski's handwriting expert would tell him they were all written by Vertiline, and no effort would be made to confirm her assertion.

Again, despair settled in her heart. Her dreadful plight seemed so inevitable, she wondered why she hadn't seen it coming years ago and done something to avoid it. As she pondered the possibilities, Vertiline found herself wondering when she had become aware that Carolee was a lost soul. *Why didn't I see that she would be the undoing of the family.*

In addition to the apartment in Brooklyn, Vertiline and her sisters rented a room above a store on Fifth Avenue in nearby Park Slope in 1902, and set out to find students for their tutoring service. They met with teachers of the local schools and were occasionally referred to a parent.

Something inexplicable stood in their way. Some of the teachers treated them as if they had a contagion. If they got as far as meeting with a parent, the reception proved similar.

Vertiline wondered if the mourning clothes the sisters wore discouraged people? Observance of the mourning ritual was less evident in Brooklyn. Did folks imagine a member of the sisters' family had died and left behind a pestilence? Was their accent, which told of the sisters' Southern origins, the problem? That would account for some of the response, but not all.

One day, when the twins were busy with other matters, Vertiline met with a teacher on her own. She experienced none of the reticence, the guarded language, and despairing looks. "A delight to meet you Miss Mortlow," Mrs. Pia said as they concluded their meeting. The conversation with the woman was delightful and warm. "Your qualifications are impressive, and we always need help from someone with your experience."

Mrs. Pia referred her to the parents of several children, and Vertiline met with some that very day. The meetings went well—Vertiline and her sisters had found their first six students.

In the afternoon two days later, they began their lessons with three students in the room over the store in Park Slope. The space had been a stock room for the haberdashery below until the shop's expansion into the first floor space toward the rear of the building. All the woodwork, including the stairs leading up to the room, was raw wood that had been stained unevenly by the touch of human hands over the years. Despite the unattractive appearance of the place, parents dropping off their children, and the students themselves, seemed to make allowances for the low-budget enterprise.

Vertiline had just finished with her student when her attention was drawn by an outburst from the back of the room where Carolee worked with a child named Elsie on English composition.

"What's wrong with you?" Carolee said to the ten-year-old girl, her tone unnecessarily cruel. "I don't care what you've learned in school. If you had learned it, you wouldn't be here. You'll conform to my methods while under my tutelage or you'll be sent home." Vertiline knew the look in Carolee's eyes would have frightened an adult.

Elsie began to cry.

Vertiline saw Mary's student, a male of about twelve, look at Carolee with apprehension.

Carolee would sabotage their efforts if Vertiline didn't step in. She drew Carolee aside. "You can't treat the children that way," Vertiline said, trying to sound reasonable, but boiling mad inside. "You must be more patient."

Carolee turned on her with fire in her eyes. "I will not stand for the brat's willful ignorance," she said, "and her blubbering." She turned back to the girl. "Pack up your things and get out!"

"Elsie must remain until her parent comes to collect her," Vertiline said evenly. She stared Carolee down, then sat consoling Elsie until the child's mother arrived.

Occasionally glaring at and Elsie, Carolee spent the time putting away supplies and straightening the room. She was out of control. Vertiline almost sent her home, but decided to see how their evening session went. One way or another, Vertiline was determined to have a long talk with Carolee when they got home.

During the evening session, Carolee struck one of the male teen-aged students who tried to argue a matter of opinion. The boy, a sixteen-year-old capable of making his own way home, fled down the stairs and out of the building.

Taking Carolee roughly by the arm, Vertiline loomed over her with a menacing expression and backed her younger sister into a corner. "That will be enough," she said. "Leave now."

Carolee, her lips pressed tightly together, stood for a moment staring at her older sister. Then she shook her arm loose and left the building.

When they lost four of the six new students after the first few sessions, Vertiline knew that Carolee's presence had created problems in starting up their tutoring service. She intimidated the adults, and the children were afraid of her. How had Vertiline not noticed it before?

Because Carolee's thinking was less focused and she had more difficulty expressing ideas, she'd been held in reserve at the college or given primarily disciplinarian roles. In a classroom filled with students at the college, she was adequate, but teaching singly, as they did currently, her manner was too aggressive.

Then a realization had gripped Vertiline; she'd put children in the care of a murderess! She'd known in her heart about her sister's anger and crimes. But she had been unwilling to face the truth because, if Carolee had such a terrible thing inside her, and there seemed no doubt that she did, Vertiline had fed it to her.

In hindsight, she thought that should have been the moment she realized Carolee would eventually destroy them all. Since Vertiline had been charged by her father with protecting the twins, she should have seen that incident as cause for immediate concern, but at the time, she was in the habit of considering only threats from outside the family. Because Vertiline suspected Mary of wrong-doing as well, and felt responsible for whatever crimes the twins committed, the blame for Carolee's behavior had been spread thinly enough that she didn't see it clearly. Vertiline had continued to deny the long term threat it posed.

She'd simply relieved Carolee of her teaching role within the tutoring business. Carolee seemed perfectly happy for her two sisters to do all the teaching, but then there had been difficulty finding enough work to keep her busy.

"Carolee does not pull her own weight," Mary complained.

"She frightens the students away," Vertiline said.

Mary seemed to understand without further explanation and didn't bring the subject up again. Still, she seemed unhappy with the distribution of work and was always looking for extra duties for Carolee to take on. Vertiline watched and worried as tension between the twins grew.

Vertiline wondered if the guards had forgotten they'd brought her back down to the Tombs. While no one was looking, she lowered her head to the surface of the table and rested.

Chapter 15
Carolee—Unknown

Carolee panicked as she felt Mary slipping away. As if Carolee were a patient who'd awakened to face the imminent amputation of a limb, she fought savagely against reality. She screamed, bleated, bounced off the walls, clutched at the air to her right, then her left, attempting to retrieve the once conjoined but presently departing personality of her sister. As the last few threads of emotional tissue parted in the swift and brutal amputation, there was a traumatic rending and a snap. Carolee was free and terribly alone in the world.

She collapsed to the floor of her cell and wept until her tears ran dry, all the while searching her own mind and body for anything that might remain of her sister. Until the present, Carolee had not realized that her twin had always stood right next to her and yet partly within her, regardless of where Mary had physically been. The general location was presently known only by the contrast of her sudden absence from it. In the place once occupied by Mary, nothing existed but a numbing cold.

Carolee's heart split in two, and she knew she'd loved Mary. Going on without her was an impossibility. How would Carolee think things through? Without an additional opinion, how could she trust herself?

Before their arrest, they'd been in New Jersey for about two months. Prior to that, during the years they spent in Brooklyn, the twins had felt more distant from each other than ever before, while living in the most cramped conditions they'd experienced since the War. Mary's nearly constant presence in that period had been a growing source of irritation, as was a frequent confusion concerning whose feelings Carolee experienced. Carolee would do it all again, though, if only she could have her sister back.

⚓

The move from Virginia to Brooklyn was difficult for Carolee, but once settled in, she came to like the big city. She understood life in Brooklyn in ways that her sisters did not. She knew that since so many people lived so closely together in the city, maintaining a proper outward appearance and presence meant something different. The attitude and movement of the body, the tilt and focus of the head and eyes, were important aspects of projecting the confidence needed to get to one's destinations, interact with people or avoid them, and stay safe while walking the streets of the city.

Carolee had never seen so much brick and stone. The Earth itself, as far as the eye could see, was nearly covered by buildings and streets, with little green remaining.

New odors abounded. Exotic and enticing aromas came from the windows of countless kitchens belonging to people from many different parts of the world. Because of the closeness of the environment and its inhabitants, other unpleasant, but familiar odors were ubiquitous; the smell of unwashed bodies, of human and animal waste, and the odors of decay, mold, and fermentation. With the abundance of horse manure in the streets, flies bred in profusion and got into everything. The drinking water was clouded with a white sediment and had a flavor suggestive of the smell of rain on hot limestone.

Seeing the wide variety of human shapes, colors, countenances, and their vast array of personalities, mannerisms, fashions, languages, and gestures, was a revelation to Carolee. She found the unfamiliar kinds of human beings intimidating until she began to see the animal in them. Then they weren't so dissimilar to herself, merely products of different backgrounds.

The sisters wore modest crepe mourning clothes with a minimum of lace, and caps with veils, which gave them a grace period when they first moved into their new neighborhood. Those who lived in the tenement or on the same street, gave simple greetings and nodded their heads toward the sisters to acknowledge their presence, but no more. Carolee and her sisters responded curtly, establishing that they were not to be disturbed. At first, perhaps out of respect for a presumed loss the sisters had suffered, neighbors allowed the distance without question, but with time and growing familiarity, they seemed to resent their presence.

The sisters' apartment was two bedrooms, a common room, and a kitchen, with pressed tin ceilings and crude cloth on the walls instead of wallpaper. The kitchen had a small iron stove and, oddly, a hung sash window in the wall that separated the cooking area from the common room. They furnished the apartment with simple beds, chairs, and a table, all bought secondhand. Fletcher and Orphia shared the bed in one room, while two beds were crammed into the other for the sisters. Mary and Carolee shared one, Vertiline took the other. The family was used to much nicer and cleaner living arrangements, but no one complained. Although Carolee appreciated two improvements over homes they'd had in the past, a water-closet and a sink in the hall outside their apartment, she was irritated by having to share them with the other tenants living on the same floor.

In the summer of 1901, shortly after moving in, while Fletcher and Orphia were gone to market for groceries, Carolee had the first of many meetings with her sisters at the table in the common room.

After they discussed the implications of the news that Orphia had become pregnant, Vertiline changed the subject. "We are few among many in a busy city. That does not mean we can do whatever we want with impunity. There's much crime here and the police have their hands full, but we will not tempt fate." She gave the twins hard looks, but especially Carolee, who was not pleased with the extra attention.

Clearly Vertiline assumed Carolee would commit further crimes and had brought her to the city so her actions might be lost in a crowd. Such misdeeds, however, were the farthest thing from Carolee's mind. If living on the run in such cramped quarters were the consequences of breaking the law, the lesson was learned.

"We could rent much better," Vertiline said, "but we need to save our money until we have an income. With Orphia's child on the way, Fletcher will have to make a significant contribution. He should find a job with all due haste."

Vertiline made eye contact with each of the twins in turn. "We can offer tutoring. We'll find a suitable room in a nice neighborhood to take in students. Then we should come up with a more ambitious plan for our continued prosperity."

"Perhaps we could open a boarding house," Mary said.

Vertiline raised an eyebrow as she considered the idea.

Too busy resenting Vertiline's attitude of distrust, Carolee wasn't interested in making plans for the future.

<hr />

Carolee met Mrs. Biermann upon answering a knock on the apartment door. The German woman, mother of five, and widow of a stevedore who died in an accident on the docks, lived in the apartment down the hall. Following awkward introductions resulting from a clash of accents, Mrs. Biermann said, "Please come for a visit next door. I have delicious jasmine tea."

Carolee was about to tell the woman to go away, but Mary joined them at the door and introduced herself. "That sounds delightful, Mrs. Biermann."

"I have beautiful dresses for sale," the woman said. "You would enjoy seeing them."

"You are here to sell us something?" Carolee asked curtly.

"My apartment is a dress shop," Mrs. Biermann said, her smile fragile, uncertain. "I make beautiful dresses."

"That's no way for neighbors to become acquainted," Carolee said.

"It's how I earn my keep," the woman replied.

Mary turned away and left her twin at the door with the woman.

"I apologize—" Mrs. Biermann was saying, but Carolee shut the door, cutting off her words.

Mary treated the rest of neighborhood to similar haughtiness. Although largely hidden beneath her veil, Carolee's gaze unnerved the neighbors. She enjoyed staring them down.

With the confusion of identity resulting from the similarity of their features and clothing, all three sisters quickly became universally despised.

The sisters found a room above a store in nearby Park Slope and began their tutoring service, but finding students was more difficult than anticipated. Money became tight and everyone but Orphia was expected to help out.

Carolee saw Fletcher as weak. He had difficulty looking people in the eye when in conversation, which did not engender confidence or trust. Although he applied and was interviewed for many teaching positions, no one hired him. Finally, he found employment in labor, but could not keep the positions.

"I'm not capable of maintaining the level of exertion necessary to work at the ship yard," he told Vertiline after quitting his seventh job. "And the men don't like me. They treat me poorly. I'm afraid of them."

"Your wife and child must depend on you to earn a living," Vertiline said, her features stern. "You must be brave and stand up to the hardships of life, defend your own, suffer the blows, and keep going. I never would have thought that a male member of my family would act so. Where's your gumption, your resolve, your manly qualities?"

Vertiline had badgered him similarly for each of his employment failures. Carolee suspected Fletcher was as afraid of her older sister as he had been of the men at the ship yard. He turned toward Orphia. She nodded and smiled in sympathy and his harried features softened.

Orphia looked groggy from the laudanum given to her by her physician, Dr. Casby, for pain during the late stages of her pregnancy. Carolee thought her daughter appeared too thin for a pregnant woman. Orphia often would not eat.

"We need to depend on you, too" Vertiline continued. "Your poor wife has endured such pain lately. The frequent visits from Dr. Casby and her medication are an expensive burden on our household finances."

"I'll find another job tomorrow," Fletcher said, "and this time, I'll stick with it." He pressed his lips into a grim line for a moment, then seemed to relax.

Fletcher displayed an exceptionally good mood as the evening meal of boiled chicken, potatoes, and cabbage was served. Again, Orphia refused food, but they were having such a pleasant evening together, no one seemed willing to argue with her and spoil the mood.

No doubt Fletcher's good mood came from certain decisions he made that evening because the next day, he didn't return from his job search. By the spring of 1902, when Orphia gave birth to Alberta, Carolee figured he was long gone.

⤛⤜

A year later, in 1903, Orphia continued to complain of the same pains experienced while pregnant and still took her medication several times a day. She ate little. Despondent over the loss of her husband and uninterested in her infant, she spent most of her time in bed, reading and napping, her child crying in her basinet nearby. The delightful young woman was no more. Carolee suspected her daughter's complaints of illness were all lies.

Dr. Casby, a tall man in his forties, with a sober face, close-cropped brown hair, and short goatee, didn't believe that. "Your daughter, Mrs. Marshall, is experiencing a chronic pain, the source of which is difficult to locate and treat." He'd said that at the end of one of his house calls. "But I will rid her of it eventually. Until then, she must remain in bed and take her medication if she's to become well again."

"Thank you for your efforts," Carolee said mechanically.

Dr. Casby produced a nearly imperceptible smile. He paused before leaving the apartment. "I must say to you, Mrs. Marshall, seeing Orphia gives me something to look forward to each week. You have—" He paused again, perhaps choosing his words carefully, his unreadable face a vexation for Carolee. "—an extraordinary daughter."

"Thank you, Dr. Casby." Carolee said, unsure what to make of him. "I hope anticipating the termination of your visits will not deter you from finding her cure."

"Of course not," he said flatly. "I want nothing more than to see the beautiful, young Orphia on her feet again." He delivered the word "beautiful" as a thing observed—not felt. He paused again with what might have been the slightest indication of embarrassment. "Is there no word from her husband?"

"No," Carolee said, confused that he spoke with words that suggested his emotions, yet displayed little of it in his bearing.

He nodded slightly, with an expression so subtle Carolee couldn't

115

quite decide if he was smiling in response to the news. His words suggested he cared about Orphia while his features tried to hide the evidence. As the doctor left the apartment, Carolee had the lingering impression that he did indeed have feelings for her daughter, but that he had difficulty expressing them.

Carolee suspected Orphia continued to complain of the pain because the medication provided a euphoric feeling and allowed her to forget her troubles. She showed no indication that she had feelings for Dr. Casby. The bills for his visits and the medication had become an increasing burden.

The sisters weren't getting much sleep because of the restless infant. Of all of them, Mary spent the most time trying to calm the child, but her efforts did little good. The only occasions when Alberta didn't cry were during her feedings. The sisters used a meat grinder to create a paste of cooked meats and vegetables for the child. Alberta grew fat.

Carolee struggled daily with her disgust for her daughter, and finally thought of a way that Orphia might become an asset.

During the next meeting at the table in the common room with her sisters, Carolee said, "I believe it's possible for Mary to persuade Orphia to commit suicide. We could insure her life and reap the benefit. She's worse than useless as she is."

Vertiline's brow lifted and her eyes widened. She stared at Carolee for a long moment. What calculations occurred behind the older sister's eyes were a mystery to Carolee. For her, the equation was simple, involving a family member's usefulness weighed against their consumption of resources.

Vertiline finally blinked and became solemn. "Orphia was such a beautiful, capable young woman. Apparently, heartache can steal the soul."

"Not the soul," Mary said, "just the desire for life."

Carolee rolled her eyes.

"I do believe I could persuade her." Mary sounded willing, but Carolee sensed a certain reluctance.

"Before you do," she said. "I must prevail upon her to give Alberta up for adoption."

Vertiline folded her hands. "I'll take out a life insurance policy on her right away, perhaps several. We'll need a certificate of health from the doctor before I can do that. Once we have a policy, she can take her own life right away if the suicide is made to look like an accident. The violence of such an act might be too discouraging, however. If she waits for two years from the start of the policy, the insurers will cover suicide."

The first step in their plan wasn't difficult, for Orphia cared nothing for the child. Alberta was given over to the Embracing Arms Asylum for Unwanted Children in the summer.

After she was gone, Carolee expected Orphia would leave her sick bed, but she did not.

"You must get up and contribute to the household," Carolee told her.

"I can't, Mother," Orphia said, the look in her eyes almost persuasive. "The pain! Please give me a little more time. The doctor says he's willing to provide the medication for free, he'll cut his visit fee to a minimum, and will provide the certificate of health you requested if he can come after hours, between seven o'clock and nine o'clock in the evening."

Those were precisely the hours the sisters provided tutoring for older students. Those were the only sessions with which Carolee was trusted to help; the only time all three sisters were away from home. Suspecting that Dr. Casby intended to do more than merely administer to Orphia's ailment, Carolee saw advantages to allowing them the privacy. She hoped the doctor's interest in the young woman was more than mere lust.

"I don't care if you intend to have sexual intercourse with him," Carolee said.

Her daughter's eyes became wide despite her grogginess under the influence of the laudanum, but she chewed her lip and said nothing.

"You are quite beautiful, if rawboned, and he's a single man. He might fall for you, help you get a divorce, and ask for your hand in marriage. That's more likely to happen, however, if you stop taking the medicine that puts you half way to sleep."

Orphia's mouth hung open, but again she said nothing. Carolee left her that way and walked out of the room.

At her meeting with her sisters that evening, Carolee said, "Dr. Casby might have feelings for Orphia. Let's give their relationship time to develop. He's a single man with a good income. We could benefit. If it doesn't work, we'll always have the insurance policies."

Her sisters agreed.

A week later, Carolee gave Vertiline the certificate of health Dr. Casby produced for Orphia.

❦

In the fall of 1904, Orphia informed her mother that she was pregnant again. Carolee sat down with her sisters to talk about it.

"Her doctor is the father, of course," she said.

"We must compel him to marry her then," Mary said. "There's truly no other way."

"Orphia hasn't divorced her husband," Vertiline said. "We have no way to determine if he still lives."

"No one has to know," Carolee said. "He could be told she's divorced Fletcher."

"No," Vertiline said. "Fletcher might come back. Surely the doctor knows he's the father, but we have no way to prove it. We must be careful. If Dr. Casby is confronted about the pregnancy, he may never return."

"Give it time," Carolee said. "That he told me about his feelings for her, although he did so in an odd manner, indicates there's something more than lust. He's quite devoted to his patient. The evidence in the bedclothes suggests that his desire for her grows by the day."

Mary turned away in disgust.

"You've known they were having sexual congress?" Vertiline said.

"Don't pretend you didn't," Carolee said, glaring at her older sister. "You take command of everything but what you find inconvenient. Then, when I take that in hand, you don't like my solutions. I may have made some bad decisions, but at least I've been honest about what needs to be done. And, yes, I'm also referring to what happened with Mr. Wilder in Christiansboro."

Speechless, Vertiline stared at Carolee for a moment, her expression one of surprise. When the older sister finally spoke, her tone was conciliatory. "I know you have had most of the responsibilities here at home while we've been teaching. I've had my suspicions about Dr. Casby, but I believed you had it well in hand. Apparently you've decided his interest in your daughter is worth the risk. I can see your point of view and I add my support to your decision."

Vertiline had never backed down like that before. Carolee liked the feeling of victory over her sister and pressed her advantage. "Yes, but you don't trust me, and you make that clear although I've done nothing since we came here to cause concern or alarm. I deserve respect and I mean to have it."

Vertiline frowned. "Please Carolee, I have only our best interests at heart. I think you know that."

"Of course she does," Mary said, a somewhat panicked look in her eyes.

Carolee wasn't willing to let the matter go. She stood, a table knife held absentmindedly in her hand, and leaned across the small table to put her face close to Vertiline's. "You, too, have made bad decisions." Briefly, as she spoke, Carolee wondered what she intended to do with the knife, and thought it would be satisfying to thrust it into her older sister.

"You married me off to a man who molested me. It was not worth the ten thousand dollars we earned upon his death. We spent years trying to make that rundown college a success, and all the while it was destined to fail. You changed Grandmother's will so we would inherit that burden."

Mary tried to pull her back, but Carolee shrugged her off.

Vertiline didn't retreat an inch. She remained seated, rigid as steel. "Father charged me with keeping you two safe."

"That's because we were children!" Carolee cried. The hand holding the knife shook.

"And as an adult, have you acted responsibly?" Vertiline spat. "Did you end your husband's life and bring a blackmailer to our doorstep?"

"I was defending myself. I was trying to do what was right."

Now, Carolee told herself, *do it!*

But her twin took a hard grip on the hand holding the knife.

Upon feeling Mary's touch, Carolee was horrified at what she'd almost done. She allowed Mary to take the knife away.

"What is right and wrong often cannot be known until it's too late," Mary said in a tone meant to soothe and calm.

The older sister's eyes were still locked on Carolee's. Had Vertiline missed the drama with the knife? *Perhaps she will never know how close she came to peril,* Carolee thought. She withdrew slowly.

Vertiline swallowed hard, took a deep breath, and then sagged in her seat. Finally she took her eyes off Carolee to look at Mary.

Carolee sat back down, shaking as she fought off her intense emotions.

"Mary's right," Vertiline said, then she added with obvious reluctance, "and…so are you. I've made mistakes and brought us trouble. I'm sorry for that. I thought I was doing right too."

Carolee's heart swelled with righteousness. She had won an argument and regained some small measure of respect from her big sister. Reflecting on the triumph, however, the smallness of the victory was painfully evident. After a lifetime together, Vertiline still saw Carolee as merely a brat and always would.

Perhaps she's right, Carolee thought, *given what I almost did to her, just now.*

No, I didn't do it! *I cannot be held responsible for what I* almost *do.*

"To survive, we have led lives of desperation," Mary said. "It's all part of *His* test."

Carolee turned on her twin. "I will not have your religion." Needing to get away from her two sisters, she shoved Mary aside, stormed from the room, and left the apartment.

119

Although hostility persisted between Carolee and Vertiline, over the following week an uneasy truce settled over the household.

⚓

"She's spotting," Doctor Casby said, "indicating there's some risk that with too much exertion she might lose the child. I recommend she remain bedridden."

Carolee had seen the blood on the bed sheets, along with his semen stains, when she gathered the linens for the wash. He was probably too rough with her, but if that was part of the appeal, the abuse must go on if the strange courtship was to continue.

⚓

Six months into Orphia's pregnancy, Dr. Casby insisted he be paid fully for his house calls again.

"We are no longer intimate," Orphia told Carolee. "He doesn't find me attractive with a swollen belly, but I must have the medication or I'll become ill."

For the remainder of her pregnancy, the sisters paid Dr. Casby for his visits and the medication. Carolee stayed home during the house calls, allowing the two no privacy.

The hot, muggy summer of 1905 arrived with the new infant. Orphia named him John. The child was underweight and wailed day and night, even right after feeding. The unhappiness in the household drove the doctor away again. Orphia's supply of laudanum ran out.

"I must have my medication," she cried, her eyes fierce with anxiety and pain. She lay in a bed soaked with sweat. "Find Dr. Casby and bring him to me or I will die!"

Carolee and her sisters each made efforts to calm her, but nothing helped. Although angry with Dr. Casby, Carolee could hardly blame him for staying away. She didn't want to be there either.

Orphia wouldn't feed her child. Mary warmed milk on the stove and sat with the bawling infant, patiently placing a few drops on his tongue when he opened his mouth to scream.

Vertiline went to fetch the doctor, but returned to say he was gone to a conference out of town and not expected back for a week.

"You must quiet John or I will have to," Orphia threatened. She stumbled about in a trance, alternately yawning and weeping. Her nose ran so profusely that the upper portion of her nightgown was soaked through. The sisters frequently brought Orphia water to drink.

Mary took the infant and a chair out into the hall of the tenement.

120

She returned much later to continue his feeding. By then Orphia's condition had worsened and she was less concerned about his crying.

"John became calm briefly and he smiled for me," Mary told Carolee, holding back a smile of her own.

Discovering a budding affection for the child beneath the words, Carolee gave her twin a questioning look.

"Much time has passed since anyone gave me more than a polite smile," Mary said, shrugging dismissively.

Carolee felt a worrisome and potentially painful need in her sister.

Over the course of the next day, Orphia began to twitch and writhe about in her bed and on the floor. "My flesh—I burn—I ache with cold."

If Orphia was to die, better for all that she'd do so quickly. The suffering was horrible to see, but for some reason Carolee could not walk away. She wondered if her twin had a hand in her staying. On occasion, Mary, perhaps unaware of what she was doing, imposed her feelings and desires on Carolee. When that happened, distinguishing between what was hers and what belonged to Mary became nearly impossible.

Carolee found herself holding her daughter, trying to contain her movements. Orphia struck out involuntarily with her limbs. Her skin took on an angry pink color and became hot to the touch. Vertiline kept insisting Orphia take more water and a little food, but abdominal cramping would not allow Orphia to keep anything solid down.

"She will surely die if we don't take her to the hospital," Mary said. Her eyes and open mouth strained with worry.

"We have three life insurance policies on her," Vertiline said. "There's no waiting period for coverage of death by illness."

Mary thought about that, nodding. She sat down with the crying infant in her lap and rocked him gently. Clearly, Mary had succumbed to an affection for the child.

Although Carolee was reconciled to the loss of her daughter, she could not take the suffering—not because she didn't want Orphia to experience the agony, but because while watching it, she, herself, felt a shade of the pain. Carolee wondered if the sympathetic reaction she felt came into her mind from Mary. Whatever the source, she could not leave her daughter. She stayed with Orphia through the night, bathing her forehead with a cool, damp cloth when the young woman became hot, and tucking her into the bedclothes when she was cold.

The next few days bled together into one long, agonizing struggle with the failures of the flesh. Orphia's symptoms worsened, and new ones emerged; liquid diarrhea, racing pulse, endless vomiting.

Orphia did not die. Eventually her symptoms subsided, but not her desire for the drug.

Carolee did her best to ignore the powerful relief she felt when the worst was over. She had feared throughout the experience that it stimulated something she did not want: Positive feelings toward her daughter.

When events in the household calmed down enough, the sisters had another meeting.

"Mary," Vertiline began, then paused as if approaching a delicate subject, "It has now been just over two years since I took out the life insurance policies on Orphia. At this time, an apparent suicide would be covered by the policies. You could begin your discussion with her while she's vulnerable to arguments for taking her own life. An easy, painless method could be employed."

Mary appeared somewhat troubled by the suggestion, but nodded her head and changed the subject. "Our funds diminish faster than they are replenished," she said. "If we're in agreement concerning the plan to open a boarding house, I suggest there's no time to waste. Has your search for an attorney borne fruit?"

"I've located one in Newark, New Jersey," Vertiline said, "where real estate prices are more within our reach. I'll make arrangements to travel to meet with him, and hopefully begin the process right away. While I'm gone to New Jersey, Mary will take charge of the household."

She turned to Carolee with a stern expression and opened her mouth to say something, no doubt an admonishment against bad behavior. Carolee was sick of being treated like a child.

Then Vertiline's features softened. "I'm sure you two will take care of things properly while I'm gone."

Another small victory perhaps, but Carolee hid her delight.

Vertiline caught a train to Newark six days later, at the end of July.

In the three weeks after Vertiline left for New Jersey, events within the household quieted. Orphia remained in bed, her emotional state desolate. Mary continued to take care of the infant, except when she tutored children in the afternoon and evening. Carolee took the duty of infant care while her twin worked. The child remained hopelessly small, but slept more regularly. When he was asleep, Mary placed him in the basinet beside Orphia.

"He will only awaken her when he starts to cry," Carolee said.

"Yes, but she might take to him if he's close," Mary said.

"And what good does that do if Orphia is going to end her life and we give the child up for adoption as planned?"

Carolee could tell that Mary's feelings for the infant, and perhaps for Orphia, left her somewhat confused. Even so, Mary nodded in agreement.

A letter arrived from Vertiline:

Bainbridge Hotel, Newark, New Jersey
August 12th, 1905

My Dear Sisters,

With the help of our attorney, Mr. Henry Galbraith, the search for a house is underway and I have hope of finding a suitable property within a month or two.

I trust all is well at home and that Mary's conversation with Orphia is productive.

Yours in urgency,
Vertiline Mortlow

Mary's discussions with Orphia concerning suicide began the fourth week after Vertiline's departure. Carolee didn't want to hear what her twin said. She recognized the tone of the murmuring voice coming through the wall and door as one of consoling, and could also feel the effect the words had on her sister. Mary quickly became unhappy with her role. She struggled to communicate only the truth, and much of what she presented was an expression of her spiritual concerns. Mary spent many hours talking to Orphia while the young woman lay in her bed unresponsive. She could have been asleep much of the time. Mary held the infant and took the time to feed him and change his diaper while in the room.

In the beginning of September the tone changed from consoling to one of counseling. Carolee knew Mary told Orphia of the three life insurance policies that had been taken out in her name, and how the family's poor financial state would benefit from the payout.

One afternoon, the door to her daughter's room was opened a crack, and Carolee heard her sister talking. Mary told of Mr. Mortlow's starvation during the war.

"He knew there wasn't enough for all of us. I believe the Almighty inspired him to make the sacrifice that allowed us to live. He had to be willing, however. You would not be here, none of us would, if he had not given everything to ensure our family's survival. Our experience during the war proves the power of such a simple, but profound, gesture."

A pause occurred—Mary was unhappy that what she intended to say next would be a lie.

"My brave son, James, made the sacrifice. The funds from his life insurance policy kept us going for many years. He's respected and remembered by all of us for his selfless act."

Another pause.

"The Lord will forgive you. You have but to—"

Carolee pushed the door closed so she wouldn't have to hear any more. Still, she heard the murmur of Orphia's voice and weeping, which indicated that the young woman was finally engaged in the conversation.

Orphia wrote several suicide notes over the next few weeks. As if the notes were meant to console, she wrote of the method of suicide by which her life would be taken, describing it as quick and painless. Apparently she considered cutting her wrists, hanging, leaping from the Brooklyn Bridge, and finding a pistol and shooting herself in the heart. Each time she failed to follow through with a plan, Mary took the newest note and saved it.

"I'm keeping them for you in case you change your mind," she told Orphia. Mary put them in a leather correspondence folio Winifred had given to Vertiline for Christmas one year. Carolee was aware that some degree of anger drove Mary to store them there, with the idea that Vertiline might find the notes and read them. Apparently Mary had resentment toward Vertiline as well.

━━◆━━

"What with my discussions with Orphia and seeing to little John's needs," Mary said to Carolee, "I have no time left. I need your help."

"What would you have me do?" Carolee asked.

"Take on the tutoring. Go to Park Slope and teach our students. Vertiline doesn't have to know."

"Yes I will, of course," Carolee said, "but what does she have to do with it?"

"She's concerned that you frighten the students."

"That's absurd."

"No, it's true. You're too hard on them and we can ill afford to lose clients."

Carolee could see the truth even as her twin spoke.

"Pretend you're someone who is pained when offending others," Mary suggested.

"I'll try."

"I'll be with you," Mary told her.

Carolee took up the duty, and was proud that she didn't lose a single client, although having to smile and appear interested in what the brats had to say was all but insufferable.

Another letter arrived from Vertiline:

Bainbridge Hotel, Newark, New Jersey
September 29th, 1905

My Dear Sisters,

I have located and purchased a property in East Orange, New Jersey. The house is large enough for our purposes, having ten rooms and a basement that can be outfitted as an apartment for the three of us. Because the structure has some damage, the price was good. I have secured the services of a carpenter and a trim carpenter to effect repairs, and I anticipate their work will be completed the end of December. We should plan to remove to our new dwelling shortly after the beginning of the year.

I will stay long enough to see the work begun, and should return to Brooklyn by November 15th.

Steadfastly yours,
Vertiline Mortlow

One evening in early November, as Carolee returned home from tutoring, Mary, in a panic, met her at the streetcar stop.

"Orphia is gone," she said. "She must have taken John with her. I was napping and when I awoke—"

"Have you looked for her?"

"Everywhere. John needs to be fed. She's been gone for hours."

"There's no sense in worry. Hopefully, she'll come home."

They walked eleven blocks to their tenement and searched the area around the building. Carolee was about to suggest they go warm up in the apartment, when Orphia emerged from a door that led to the basement of the building. In her nightgown, she appeared ghostly in the light from the gas lamps on the street, her movements unsure and her features trancelike.

Mary hurried to her side. "Orphia, I was so worried."

Carolee took her time, her hips sore from riding on the hard bench in the street car.

"Where's John?" Carolee asked.

Orphia had yet to focus on Mary. She pulled away from her and headed for the front door of the building. Carolee gripped her right arm and turned her around. "*Where's your infant?*" she said.

Orphia focused on her mother. "The only way to send him to heaven—" she said.

"What are you saying?" Carolee asked.

"—Aunt Mary said…but I couldn't find another way."

"Please, Orphia," Mary said, "tell us where you've taken John."

Orphia's eyes darted about, fixing on nothing. "There were knives, and a hammer, and the window, but I couldn't do it."

Carolee ushered them inside and up the stairs to their apartment. When Orphia was in her bed, Carolee put her hands on either side of her daughter's face and turned her head. She leaned over her and asked loudly, "*Where's John?*"

Orphia cried out, her wide eyes finally focused on her mother. "Where is he?" Carolee asked quietly, but with urgency.

"To send him to Heaven, I put him in Hell." Orphia seemed confused, unsure of her location, her eyes darting again.

Mary's legs folded beneath her and she collapsed at the foot of the bed, moaning, "No... no...!"

Carolee turned to her sister. "What's wrong? What has happened?" She tried to help her stand, but Mary was unresponsive.

"I never meant she should send her child to heaven!" Mary cried.

"What do you mean?"

Propped up against the leg of the bed, Mary appeared defeated, tears streaming down her cheeks. She looked like an old version of Carolee, what Carolee would look like in another decade, lines of sorrow deeply etched in her face. "I told Orphia she'll go to Heaven when she leaves this world," Mary said. "I told her life is too hard, that it's always been a hardship for me to watch my children suffer through life, that it's a blessing for my son, James, to have gone to heaven at an early age, avoiding much suffering."

"Religious bunkum!" Carolee cried.

Mary gasped and bawled like a child. Never as an adult had she acted that way.

Wave upon wave of shame and regret crashed against Carolee's frame of mind; the self-satisfied complacency she used to protect her sense of self. At first the frame held. A mere trickle of Mary's emotion reached her. She didn't want to know or feel what her sister experienced in that moment. She didn't want to care.

Then a deluge as the protective frame began to come apart under the assault.

Carolee had to get out. She turned and fled through the door, out of the apartment, and onto the street. Still, awareness of Mary's turmoil dogged her. Although the hour was late, she fled into the night, traveling at least a mile on foot to get away from the flood of emotion, but the distance didn't help.

She saw men on the street, and knew she should fear them, but they were merely desperate creatures like herself.

They should be afraid of me, she thought briefly.

Thinking about them helped. She looked for more people.

Seeing a dead horse in an intersection ahead, she turned and moved up a street to her right. In the next blocks, a few men and women sat or stood in clusters on or around front stoops, gossiping, telling jokes, the men and a few of the women smoking. They were a slovenly bunch, but not threatening. Their presence provided some distraction from the relentless flow of Mary's emotion into Carolee.

Soon, however, exhaustion claimed her, and she looked for a place to rest for a moment. Carolee stepped into a dark alley and settled onto the gritty pavement, her back resting against a brick wall.

If Mary became exhausted and fell asleep, then I, too, could rest.

Carolee wondered if perhaps, just as her sister had done to her, she could influence Mary's state of mind. Carolee closed her eyes, tried to banish all thoughts, and to know only her feeling of exhaustion and need for sleep. She tried to project that weariness into her twin. At first, the experience was more painful, as her sister's emotions hit her without the buffer of distraction. Carolee persisted, discovering the intoxicating edges of sleepiness. With time, Mary's flood began to diminish, became a trickle again, and finally ceased.

Carolee awoke near dawn, distressed to find that she had fallen asleep and spent the night in the alley. She knew that Mary still slept. Carolee wondered if she had succeeded in putting her twin to sleep or if Mary had gone to sleep on her own.

Light was just beginning to purple the eastern sky as Carolee emerged from the alley and turned toward home. Her posterior was numb. Her back and hips ached.

When she arrived at the tenement nearly a half-hour later, she made a quick search in and around the building before going in. Again, no luck in finding the infant; she returned to the apartment.

Carolee knew that if John had been left out overnight, he had surely perished. But dead or alive, if neighbors found his tiny body, she and her sisters might suffer terrible consequences.

Most of the day, Mary and Orphia remained in bed. Carolee napped, then made another search of the tenement and the surrounding area without locating little John.

When Mary and Orphia finally awoke, they remained largely unresponsive.

"We have to find John," Carolee told her twin, shaking her.

"It's too late," Mary said in a whisper. "Don't worry, he won't be found." She knew something, but wasn't going to tell Carolee.

Even if the infant's remains didn't turn up, there were other signs of his existence. What of the neighbors? They would soon notice the crying of the infant no longer came from the apartment. The sisters had cultivated their privacy, and most of the neighbors minded their own business. The German woman down the hall and an Italian woman, Mrs. Calise, who occupied the front stoop with her little brats each day, were the exceptions. Whenever Mrs. Biermann heard the sisters in the hall, whether they were retrieving water, using the water closet or coming and going from their apartment, she opened her door and peeked out to see what was going on. Similarly, when the sisters came and went through the front door of the building, Mrs. Calise and her brood unabashedly followed them with their eyes.

If nothing was said about the loss of the baby, hopefully no one would suspect anything for a little while, but eventually someone would notice.

Carolee walked four blocks along Bedford Avenue to the Brooklyn Telegraph Office and sent a telegram to Vertiline.

VERTILINE MORTLOW
THE BAINBRIDGE HOTEL NEWARK NEW JERSEY
VERTILINE -(STOP)- COME HOME IMMEDIATELY -(STOP)-
EMERGENCY -(STOP)-
CAROLEE MORTLOW MARSHALL
4:27 PM

Vertiline did not arrive for two more days. In that time, Carolee got Mary and Orphia up and functioning in a more responsive manner. She gave them baths, made them brush their hair and teeth. When they had dressed themselves and sat down at the table, she served them food. The two downcast women drank some milk and ate a little bread and butter.

With little effort, Carolee convinced them of the necessity of moving out of the tenement to avoid suspicion. Mary and Orphia halfheartedly helped Carolee make decisions about what to pack. They filled four trunks and three valises, and decided to leave all the furniture behind. Orphia became more coherent in conversation; Mary spoke, but didn't make eye contact.

When Vertiline arrived home, Carolee apprised her of what had occurred in her absence. The older sister's eyes flashed with anger and skepticism, but she held her tongue, her eyes darting toward Mary as if seeking confirmation. Each time Mary nodded her head, but would not look directly at her. Carolee finally had had enough of Vertiline's attitude. She stopped in mid-sentence and turned away.

"What happened to the baby?" Vertiline demanded, but she clearly only wanted to hear the parts of the story that were damning to Carolee—never mind that there weren't any.

"If Carolee had not made us ready," Mary said softly, "we'd still be in bed. I was no help at all. She knew what had to be done and made us do it. She's correct when she says we have to leave before the neighbors become suspicious."

"What happened to the baby, Orphia?" Vertiline asked. She gripped her niece by the shoulders. "Where did you leave John?"

Orphia could not turn away bodily, but she turned her head and eyes as far from Vertiline as she could manage and remained silent. Her eyes were glassy and a tear spilled down her right cheek.

Vertiline raised a hand to slap the young woman.

"Leave her alone!" Carolee cried and stepped in to draw her daughter away.

Vertiline backed away and raised her hands in surrender. "I'm trying to find the truth."

"We've tried," Mary said. "She won't say, and we don't know."

Carolee knew Mary was lying, but she still didn't know the truth herself and didn't want to know.

A tense, uncomfortable silence ensued. Orphia teetered for a moment and almost fell, caught herself, and became still.

Finally, Vertiline seemed to relax. Mary relaxed too, and then Carolee was able to do the same.

"The house in East Orange isn't ready," Vertiline said. "We'll have to get another room or suite at the hotel until January."

She turned to Carolee, her features softened. "Thank you for what you did here. I know you are trying not to be so rash as you've been in the past, but we have a history together that colors my thinking. I can't help it, but it's not fair to you. I'm sorry."

Carolee could not remember the last time she'd smiled, and as her mouth widened and muscles pulled up at the corners of her lips, the expression felt a little strange, more like baring her teeth to frighten Vertiline, although that wasn't her intention.

Or was it?

In November and early December, temporary repairs were made to the house in East Orange, its damaged roof and an exterior wall above the porch "weathered-in," as the carpenter referred to it, with the use of tar-saturated roofing felt. Permanent repairs, he told them, would have to wait for warmer weather. By the first of the year, 1906, the basement apartment had been finished. Mary, Orphia, and most of the three sisters' possessions were installed there along with recently purchased second-hand furniture. Carolee wasn't surprised that her older sister claimed the largest room. Vertiline spent time arranging her possessions within it, although she didn't plan to live there for some time to come. Supplies for further repairs on the house occupied floor space in both Carolee's and Vertiline's rooms, so they kept their accommodations at the Bainbridge Hotel and slept there instead.

Carolee knew Mary and Orphia continued their conversation about suicide.

One afternoon in late January, Carolee answered a knock on her hotel room door. A young redheaded bellboy greeted her and handed her a message from the registration desk.

Mrs. Carolee Mortlow Marshall has received a telephone message from Mrs. Mary Mortlow Sneed.
Message as follows:
Mrs. Carolee Mortlow Marshall, please come immediately to the house in East Orange.

Vertiline was out, but Mary had not asked for her to come anyway. Carolee asked at the front desk for a taxi. She rode in an electric cab the three miles to the house in East Orange. The ride was rough but quiet, and she arrived quicker than anticipated.

As she approached the house, Mary met her on the walk to the door of the basement apartment. "Your sweet daughter has passed on," she whispered, her expression downcast, but also fearful.

Carolee felt a sudden hollowness in her chest. Something was gone that she hadn't expected to miss. Mary's memory of the incident was strangely opaque to her. "What happened?"

"Come inside." Mary led Carolee to the small bathroom of the basement apartment. Orphia lay on her back, naked in the half-filled tub, her head under the faucet, feet dangling over the back of the fixture.

In an instant, Carolee knew what happened, but not the details. She turned on Mary. "You killed her!" she cried, and struck her twin in the face with an open hand. She recoiled from the pain, as did her twin. She advanced on Mary again and struck two more blows, hitting her in the face with her fists. Mary didn't defend herself. Each blow took Carolee's own breath away and addled her. She could not continue the assault.

Carolee turned to leave the apartment, but Mary grabbed her about the shoulders and held her. Carolee struggled, but Mary held on and dragged her to the floor. The twins lay in a heap weeping. After a time, they found themselves hugging each other for comfort.

"Orphia finally became aware of what she'd done to her infant," Mary said. She pulled herself away from Carolee and sat with her back against the wall. "Your daughter was in a state of wretchedness I'd never known anyone to experience. She had hardly eaten anything in over a month with the hope that, like her grandfather, she would expire, oblivious and without pain, in her sleep. She could not forgive herself for what she'd done, and yet was too afraid to take her own life. Of course, you don't believe, but I knew there was only one who could forgive her and provide the release she needed, but I also knew she would not meet Him in this world."

Carolee turned to her sister and snarled hopelessly, feebly, like an animal caught in a snare; a trap of her own devising.

"Regardless of your belief, please try to understand," Mary said. "Orphia was suffering, and I could help her, so I did. I was already responsible for the death of her little one. The things I said to Orphia while trying to persuade her to take her own life led her to murder her child."

Mary's face crumpled in shame and she wept. Carolee had never felt anything so intensely and wanted only for the experience to end. The pain helped her, however, to understand why Mary had ended Orphia's life. She sat beside her twin and held her hands.

"I found a doctor," Mary said, "to give laudanum to me for a pain I professed to have in my abdomen. I went to the apothecary to fill the order and found I could buy as much as I wanted. Orphia had never lost the desire for the medication. She craved it like a drunkard craves liquor. I bought three bottles and left them out for her to find while I went to market. When I returned, as I'd hoped, she had had some—quite a lot, I think. She was barely conscious, but was smiling. She became more alert, and I encouraged her to have more laudanum."

Mary paused with a grim smile. "She told me a joke."

Outraged to hear of humor in the situation, Carolee turned away with a scowl, but Mary remained quiet long enough to pique her twin's curiosity. "Tell it to me," Carolee said.

Mary took a deep breath, smiled sadly. "A mistress asked her maid, 'Janet, how did my fine vase become broken?' The maid said, 'I'm sorry, ma'am, but I was accidentally dusting.'"

Carolee felt herself smiling sadly and saw the expression mirrored in her twin.

Then the solemn expression returned to Mary's face. "I waited until she was asleep, then put a pillow over her mouth and nose, and held it tight until she stopped breathing."

Again, the shame, but not for expected reasons—Mary had enjoyed killing Orphia. Carolee knew exactly how her sister felt.

"I put her in the bath tub to make it appear she'd drowned herself, but the stopper won't hold the water for long."

For the first time, Carolee became aware of the trickling sound coming from the bathroom, as the leaky stopper beneath Orphia's head allowed the bathtub to slowly empty.

Finally Carolee stood. She leaned over and offered her hand to help her twin stand. "Come, Mary, we have more to do."

Mary stood and retrieved an appropriately nonspecific suicide note from Vertiline's correspondence folio, and pinned the message to Orphia's clothing heaped beside the tub.

The pain and sorrow I suffer in this life are greater than I can endure. My husband left me, and my daughter was given up for adoption. My little son has died and gone to Heaven. I long to be there too. I have been ill and weak a very long time. Death will be a blessed end to my sufferings. When you read this I will be gone.

Orphia Marshall Sneed

The twins refilled the tub, disposed of the laudanum, then called on Mary's new doctor and told him that Orphia had committed suicide by drowning.

Carolee, alone as never before in her padded cell, curled into a ball on the dirty floor. She covered her eyes, trying to cease her existence and follow Mary. She would reject everything her senses offered; shut out the world and thereby, somehow, exit life and pass on with her sister. She tried to plug her ears while holding her forearms over her eyes, but she couldn't close off the flow of sounds, the various voices of patients and staff within the building, and the susurrus of their activity. A word or two, a clang of metal on metal, drew her attention. She pushed the sounds away and emptied her mind.

Relaxed, Carolee soon lost unawareness of her sore joints. She didn't feel the padding beneath her. No taste stimulated her mouth. Breath, flowing almost imperceptibly in and out of her, was odorless.

A piece of grit beneath her shoulder, a honeycomb pattern in darkened vision, a stabbing pain in an elbow, the ringing of the clock tower bell, a cockroach crawling across an ankle; each tugged at consciousness, but all were pushed away without a thought. A state of subtle emotional and mental flux occurred in which the mind held onto nothing. Finally a formless expanse opened, not perceived with the senses, but experienced by intuition alone.

Within the mysterious openness Carolee felt the presence of her twin. As she reached for Mary's spirit, Carolee's mind compared the sensation to that described by soldiers she'd met after the war who experienced phantom pains in limbs lost to amputation. Was the presence a mere phantom? Upon questioning the reality of Mary's spirit, Carolee's consciousness popped back out of the expanse.

The sensations she received from the world around her became unavoidable.

Tears flowed with a sense of failure, but also with elation, as she chose to believe her connection to Mary was not completely severed. That she'd had the thought, instead of merely an emotional response, suggested her sister indeed remained a reasoning part of her mind.

Chapter 16
Vertiline—Depression

Startled from sleep by the sound of a door opening, Vertiline recognized the room as part of the Tombs and remembered being brought there.

Mr. Hitchens entered and sat heavily at the table across from her, a weariness about his features.

"I just had a discussion with the prosecuting attorney," he said. "I told him that we would look into who wrote the essays whether he did or not. I cannot say what Mr. Kalinowski will do, but he is reassessing his strategy. He'll come shortly to meet with us."

Vertiline sat up straighter and felt herself smile, but Mr. Hitchens didn't respond to her change in mood. He seemed to have difficulty looking at her, and she wondered if he had reason to be afraid of what Mr. Kalinowski would do.

Finally, he said, "I have two pieces of sad news for you." He paused for a moment before continuing. "The first is that your house in East Orange was burned to the ground this afternoon. The suspicion is that someone unhappy with the trial set it ablaze."

Vertiline clutched at her collar, trying to loosen the fabric to allow herself more air. The house was not insured and held everything the sisters owned.

Mr. Hitchens stepped out briefly to fetch her a cup of water, then took his seat again.

"That's not the worst of it," he said with a troubled look. "Your sister, Mrs. Mary Mortlow Sneed, has passed away."

Vertiline gasped, a hollow ache opening in her chest with the sense of loss. She sagged forward and lowered her head to the table top.

"It's believed she starved herself to death."

She had failed her sister, her father!

"My condolences."

What did he know of loss? Vertiline had fought alongside her sisters since the start of The War Between the States. The culture into which Vertiline had been born was still under siege and suffering a systematic destruction. As part of that culture, Vertiline had led her sisters as if they were on the run from the enemy, avoiding detection while living in the occupied territory of Georgia and then Virginia, and, in more recent years, in the enemy territory of New York and New Jersey. Finally, because of Vertiline's mistakes, they were run to ground. She couldn't help but think of Mary as a casualty of the continuing conflict.

Her father had given her one great task in life: To take care of her sisters, but she had failed. Mary was gone. Would she lose Carolee soon too?

A knocking came from the door of the meeting room. The door opened and the prosecuting attorney entered with a guard. Mr. Kalinowski offered a document of several pages to Mr. Hitchens.

"Miss Vertiline Mortlow," he said. "You are hereby charged with obstruction of justice in the disappearance of your great nephew, John Sneed."

Orphia's infant son!

"If you plead guilty to manslaughter in the case of your niece, Mrs. Orphia Sneed, we will withdraw the new charge; drop the charges against your sister, Mrs. Carolee Mortlow Marshall; not pursue aiding and abetting charges in the disappearance of the infant against Mrs. Marshall, and recommend to the judge a sentence for you of fifteen years. If you don't accept our offer before noon Friday, the day after tomorrow, we'll continue with the trial, pursuing the original charges against Mrs. Marshall and the new charges against the both of you."

He turned to Mr. Hitchens. "I will leave you two to discuss the offer."

"Thank you," her attorney said.

Once Mr. Kalinowski was gone, Mr. Hitchens turned to her. "I didn't think the prosecution would go for the obstruction of justice and the aiding and abetting charges. They're threatening the charges as leverage because they can't prove your niece did not write the suicide notes."

Vertiline was dumbstruck. She was exhausted, beaten down by the relentless emotional strain.

"Perhaps we should discuss their offer after you've slept on it," Mr. Hitchens said.

Vertiline merely nodded her head in response.

He called for the guard to prepare her escort back to the jail.

Vertiline held her tears as she passed under guard through the gray corridors of the courthouse and out to the police van. She held them during the drive through a light drizzle back to the jail, and as she was escorted to her cell and locked in.

When finally alone, Vertiline's tears would not come. She lay on the bunk trying to think clearly despite her emotional turmoil.

The mortician, Mr. Wilder, tried to blackmail the family because he had evidence that Carolee poisoned her husband. No doubt, Carolee set Mary's son, James, ablaze. Carolee, Mary or both might have taken part in the disappearance of Orphia's infant, John. Mary most likely provided the laudanum that killed Orphia. Truly, Vertiline did not know if Mary had a hand in Carolee's earlier crimes. Mary protected her twin with silence to the end. The crimes had occurred, of that Vertiline was certain, but Mary had passed beyond the reach of the law and Carolee was possibly beyond hope.

If Vertiline had exposed the crimes of her sisters and allowed them to suffer the consequences, they would have learned. If she had suffered the consequences of her own crimes, she, too, might have learned.

Perhaps it wasn't too late. Carolee might have already learned her lesson—Vertiline had seen a change in her sister since they left Virginia. As far as she knew Carolee had not engaged in criminal acts since then. She might become well again. If Vertiline took the prosecution's offer, Carolee would still have a chance for a decent life.

But, again, wasn't that exactly the sort of thinking on Vertiline's part that had helped her sister avoid facing her crimes? She found herself with the same conundrum she'd always had. What would be protecting her the way their father intended? When it came to Carolee, it seemed the choices Vertiline had were never good.

If Vertiline left her sister to defend herself, Carolee would go to prison. If she had time to learn from the experience, perhaps that would be best for her, but at the age of fifty-nine she wasn't likely to gain an improved perspective.

No, she would only suffer.

And what about the choices Vertiline must make for herself? She was too exhausted to think about it.

Finally, she wept for the loss of Mary, for the shame of failing her father, for the waste she'd made of her own life, and the degrading future she and Carolee faced, whatever her decision.

God had not come to her aid after all.

Chapter 17
Vertiline—Revenants

Footsteps sounded along the corridor outside Vertiline's cell and a guard appeared. "You have a visitor," he said, unlocking the door.

No one had visited her since she was taken into custody except for her attorney and representatives of the state's prosecution. She wasn't inclined to visit with anyone, but curiosity got her up, and she followed the guard through the corridors to the meeting room.

An old black man sat at the table in the room. He was examining his hands, but looked up when she entered. Those eyes—she would never forget them. The face was heavily lined, but the features belonged to Merrill, who had been a slave and her father's personal servant in her childhood home.

"Hello, Miss Mortlow," he said, standing.

Vertiline's mouth went dry and her heart began to beat rapidly as a fear of remembrance gripped her. Although she'd done her best to hide the memories of the end of the War beneath a clutter of kinder, gentler, and even false reminiscences, they were too large to obscure completely. The hard, sharp edges of shame, fear, and anger associated with the recollections had always jutted from the wreckage of her past and snagged her if she came too close.

Vertiline stumbled, but the guard caught her and guided her to the seat across from Merrill as she tried to catch her breath. The old black man's silhouette against the bright far window became a dark passage into the past.

⚓

Mr. Mortlow had been asleep in his chair in the study since the Union army moved east out of Milledgeville a week earlier. Vertiline kept the blanket tucked in around him to keep out the persistent cold.

The sisters ate their last biscuits and shared the last tin of food five days ago on the second day of December. Since the rationing of food supplies had begun in September and portions made smaller and smaller with time, starvation was well underway. The twins were testy and restless for a long while, but then settled down. Lately they had slept a lot.

Wearing her father's heaviest wool coat with the cuffs rolled back, Vertiline foraged for food in the empty houses of the neighborhood after dark, searching farther and farther afield each night, but finding next to nothing. At first she was surprisingly alert and vigilant. When she discovered people, she retreated before they saw her. As she became weaker, she grew careless, nearly revealing her presence to a pair of men exiting a house she wanted to search. She became increasingly fearful of meeting up with the type of desperate men of which her father had warned.

She limited her foraging by day to an area within earshot of her house in case her father and sisters needed her. The Shannons' house was one of the first she'd searched in daylight. A first floor window had been broken, giving her relatively easy access to the interior. The three-story home appeared to have been abandoned for a long time, which made Vertiline skeptical of her father's statements that he had been communicating with Mr. Shannon. But something about the property drew her interest. She lost track of how many times she'd been there. Stumbling about, as if in a dream, she noticed a four-foot-tall, fifteen-foot-long hump in the garden behind the house. Circling the berm, she discovered an opening leading down into the ground on the side facing the privet hedge that marked the boundary between the Shannon property and that of her own home. The doorway of sorts was formed of rough masonry and darkness filled the interior. A thin vapor rose out of the opening into the frigid air.

Vertiline retrieved a lamp from the Shannon house, lit it, and peered into the darkness below the berm. The rough stonework continued within. The hump of dirt above the structure was held up by broad, flat stones that formed a ceiling supported by crude masonry side walls, and a wall that bisected the chamber. Entering and descending three steps, Vertiline found she had a choice of two directions and chose to move into the left half of the chamber.

The still and quiet within was oppressive, giving her an impression that it might be a tomb. No sound from without made its way inside the chamber, and that was troublesome. If she were smart, she'd retreat and fetch the twins. Their presence would give Vertiline courage to continue the search.

With another look, however, she'd seen the extent of the left half of the chamber; a mere ten-by-four-foot floor, the ceiling six feet above. The bedrock that formed the floor was broken toward the rear to reveal a small channel through the rock beneath. Water flowed in the channel, coming from the left and passing under the wall that bisected the chamber. In the righthand section, the channel continued across the floor and into the wall to the right. The water flowing in the channel passed out of the chamber there. The underground water, although chilly, was warmer than the wintry air, creating the vapor.

Some of the rough stones that formed the walls stuck out to provide shelves. Rings in the moistened dust on the shelves suggested that jars had been placed there at times.

The structure was a spring house! Fear fled with the realization that she'd found a place for food storage.

Disappointed with the empty shelves, she turned her attention to a hole into the interior of the wall that bisected the chamber. Vertiline pushed the rolled sleeve of her father's coat up to expose her right arm. Despite trepidation about encountering living things inside, she slid her hand into the hole and found a space within the wall to the left and right. Her hand found something in the space to the left. Carefully, she closed her fingers around the object and withdrew it from the wall. A carved wooden giraffe—a child had played in the spring house. She put her hand back in and drew out three marbles, one blue and green, another red and blue, and one solid yellow. She put them in a pocket of her father's coat.

Vertiline pushed up the other sleeve and sent her left hand into the space to the right, finding a cold, smooth shape, a vessel of some sort with a lid. Her mouth watered at the thought that she'd found preserves or pickles as she pulled a crockery jar from the opening. She leaned back against the opposite wall and lifted the lid. The light from the lamp seemed unwilling to illuminate the interior of the jar. The container looked empty. She put a hand in and felt something on the bottom cool and firm, yet moist and slippery. She lifted her hand out with some of the substance on her fingers. The stuff felt oily. She lifted the fingers to her nose. *Butter!* She licked them. *Yes, butter!*

Vertiline slid to the floor, licking her fingers greedily, and was about to devour the contents of the jar, about four tablespoons of the fat, when she thought of her sisters. She couldn't hear them if they cried for help. Knowing she should share the butter with them, she got up and exited the spring house, carrying the crockery as if it were the most precious object in the world. She passed through the hole she'd cut in the privet hedge, and made her way through the garden to her house.

When she opened the door that led into the kitchen, Vertiline heard unfamiliar male voices inside. She wanted to turn and run, but had to protect her father and sisters. Surely, when the intruders broke in, Mr. Mortlow had awakened and crawled into the hiding place with the twins.

Vertiline set the jar of butter on the steps leading up to the door, and took off her shoes and her father's coat. She carried the shoes and coat into the kitchen and hid beneath the table, listening. The voices came from upstairs and had unusual accents. A knocking sound also came down from above.

Vertiline left the coat and shoes under the table. Trying to avoid the sections of floor that squeaked, she moved through the kitchen and dining room. She took up a position in the shadow of the space underneath the flight of stairs. Light on her feet, she'd made virtually no sound.

"I know it's here somewhere." The voice seemed to come from her father's slave, Jasper. "The tins of food have chicken, I think. There's dried stuff as well, if it isn't all gone."

Vertiline almost revealed herself, wanting to call up the stairs to the slave, but her suspicion returned quickly.

"Better not be gone," said another voice with the strange accent. "If you dragged us all the way out here for nothing, you'll answer for it."

The voices, presently muffled, continued in querulous tones, followed by the sounds of a scuffle and harsh words. After a time, all was calm again and the knocking resumed. Recognizable by their squeak, the drawers of Mr. Mortlow's desk were opened. Something toppled over with a loud crash.

Then came a battering sound as of heavy wood colliding with a wall, followed by the muffled screams of the twins.

"It came from inside the wall," Jasper's voice said.

Vertiline moved up the stairs without making a sound, crouched behind the newel post, and peeked around the banister.

Mr. Mortlow lay on the floor beside his upset chair. Had they killed him? Beyond him, four men in blue Yankee uniforms inspected the wall of the study. She saw the young black man, Jasper. He looked thinner than she remembered him. He crouched beside the wall, running a hand along the wainscoting. They would find the catch to the panel that opened into the hiding place any moment. She must stop them.

"Over here!" Vertiline shouted, standing up. The intruders turned toward her and her heart leapt into her throat. She had a burst of energy, like nothing she'd had in months, and could hardly keep up with her legs as she turned and dashed down the stairs, half stumbling.

"Gragston," a voice shouted, "get her!"

Vertiline heard a single set of heavy steps—only one of the men followed!

Her legs under control again, but aching from the exertion, she ran back through the dining room. She turned left out of the kitchen into the short hall that led to the servant's quarters, crouched against the wall, and became still.

The soldier, running into the kitchen, must have seen the back door open and assumed she'd left the house. Moving fast, he passed through the door. The sound of the butter jar crashing, breaking against the stones that paved the ground outside the door, was followed by a heavy thud, a whoosh as of breath suddenly expelled, and a series of moans.

Vertiline moved to the door and peeked out. The soldier was collecting himself and rising. He glanced up and saw her.

"Stop, girl!" he shouted.

Vertiline turned. The burst of energy was gone and her legs were sluggish as she moved toward the front of the house and blundered into the arms of another soldier in the dining room. He grabbed her by the right arm, spun her around, and slipped his left arm around her neck. She tried to kick backwards and stomp his feet, but her legs were weak and she couldn't land a solid blow. He pulled her arm up behind her back so painfully that she was forced to cease struggling. He let go with his left hand, and then she was addled by a blow of something hard against her head. She fell to the floor. The soldier stood above her, holding his pistol in his left hand.

She wondered if she had been shot, but had no time to decide.

Vertiline awoke to Jasper's screams. She found herself in the parlor, lying on the settee. Relieved to see that no one watched her, she tried to remain still and quiet.

Carolee sat on the floor, tied hands to feet, a vicious look in her eyes. Mary sat in a chair, shaking with fear and perhaps from the cold, but otherwise unencumbered. The temperature had risen slightly, but dressed in the simple light blue shifts they'd worn for over a week, the twins were no doubt freezing, as was Vertiline.

Looking over at her big sister, Mary's eyes became wide. She opened her mouth, but Vertiline put her finger to her lips as a signal for silence.

Rifles leaned against the wall in the corner. A pistol sat atop the credenza beside the door.

Jasper was tied to the door that led into the hall. The soldiers took turns beating him, except for Gragston, the one who had chased Vertiline. A young blonde fellow with a scraggly beard, he sat slumped in a chair nursing his right forearm, and licking a shard of the butter crockery. All the soldiers wore the insignia of privates except for one with the chevrons of a corporal.

Jasper's left wrist was tied to the knob and his right one tied to the upper door hinge. With each blow of a soldier's fist to Jasper's gut, ribs or face, the black man let out a hoarse cry and the door swung closed a little. The rope through the doorjamb caused it to bounce back open.

Although clearly Jasper led the soldiers to the house with a promise of hidden food, Vertiline didn't want him to suffer. She cringed with each blow. Jasper was a good, compassionate sort of man, one with healing skills. Her father had hired him out to other households to treat suffering slaves and livestock.

What of her father? Was he lying dead upstairs? The soldiers' seeming lack of concern for anything outside the room suggested her father wasn't a threat.

A blow to Jasper's face knocked teeth out. As they clattered to the floor, Mary let out a sharp cry.

One of the soldiers turned his attention to her. He was middle-aged, dark, and hirsute. "You're next, little girl," he said with a cruel smile.

Mary bent herself into the cushions of the chair. She glanced at her big sister, but Vertiline pretended unconsciousness, watching what happened through the slightest opening of her eyelids. Mary turned away, put her hands together in prayer and mouthed words silently.

"But don't worry none," the hirsute one continued, "I got something a little softer to beat you with."

"Something softer, old man?" the soldier beside him said, slapping him on the shoulder. "What you got, a limp plug tail? That's no way to treat a fine young lady. She'll want the arborvitae." He rubbed the crotch of his sweat-stained, pale blue trousers. His large nose ran, and his eyes were cold and devoid of emotion despite his attempt at humor.

His words seemed to get the men thinking about other matters. They left Jasper, turning toward the sisters. The corporal reached for Mary with hands smeared in Jasper's blood.

She screamed.

"Take me," Vertiline shouted, sitting up suddenly. "She's just a girl."

The corporal turned toward Vertiline, abandoning Mary.

The soldier referred to as having a limp plug tail took his place.

"Don't let them hurt us, Vertiline," Mary said.

Limp Plug Tail laughed.

Carolee growled as the soldier who spoke of arborvitae sized her up, then she bared her teeth. He took a step back, his eyes wide with surprise around his big nose.

"Vertiline, is it?" the corporal said. He was tall and strong in appearance, despite a thin frame, and had oily brown hair plastered to his head. "Such a pretty name for such a homely young woman."

"All of them are scrawny girls," said Arborvitae with a boyish giggle that seemed horribly out of place.

The corporal was filthy in a manner Vertiline had never seen before. Blackness, perhaps soot, rubbed into the seams and pores of his weathered skin, and a shine of cooled sweat, as if he'd suffered an illness and not washed since, gave his features a frightfully vivid gleam in the bright light coming from the windows. The miasma of odors coming from him became so powerful as he came close, Vertiline's throat seized several times in a gag reflex.

"I'm not so handsome myself, right now," he said. "We'll just agree not to look at each other. How would that be?"

Vertiline didn't answer. He sat on the settee and pushed her back.

She wanted to hate him, but didn't think of him as human. She couldn't hate an animal, but she could fear one.

Limp Plug Tail was on top of Mary. She struggled while he pressed his hairy mouth against hers and clutched at her chest.

Arborvitae was circling Carolee.

"Just knock her senseless," Gragston told him.

The corporal slipped his right hand under Vertiline's skirts and began working his way through the complex of fabrics to her crotch. His eyes told her that if she resisted, she and her sisters would suffer.

Still, Vertiline pressed her knees tightly together. She'd lost so much weight, though, the effort did little to stop the progress of his hand.

With his other hand, he ripped open her blouse and undergarments to expose her breasts.

Her only chance was to get to the credenza and pick up the pistol, which was much like the one her father had shown her how to use. She tried to imagine holding, aiming, and firing it. Vertiline thought she could do it.

The corporal worked his fingers between the lips of her vagina. She knew the digits belonged to a man capable of inflicting great pain. That they were smeared with Jasper's blood was bad enough, but she couldn't help wondering what other vile product of the war he would leave inside her.

This isn't a true experience, she told herself. Somehow, she'd failed to awaken from a nightmare—that was all. But the vivid sensations argued against her imagination's assertion.

To survive and save my sisters, I must not FEEL ANYTHING!

When his finger penetrated her vagina, she cried out, but pushed away the shame, the humiliation, an agonizing powerlessness, a sense of failure, and the crushing death of what she had dreamed sexual intimacy might become for her one day with the right man.

She squeezed her eyes closed though she failed to shut it all out. Allowing that the molestation was real, still she might survive the event. To do so, she must let go of her sense of self, of time, and place. She was trying to leave her own body when Carolee screamed.

Vertiline opened her eyes to see her sister lunge with her teeth at Arborvitae. He was so startled, he fell over backwards. All eyes turned in their direction. Arborvitae punched Carolee in the side of the head, and she rolled off to his left.

Vertiline saw Merrill standing in the doorway, holding the pistol from the credenza, right before his deep voice roared. "This pistol has one for each of you and two for good measure."

The Yankees stared dumbstruck at Merrill as he trained the pistol on each of them in turn. He was thin and haggard, but stood tall with a fierce expression. With his left hand, he used a knife to cut Jasper down. When the beaten black man hit the floor, Arborvitae leapt up to attack. Merrill aimed effortlessly and shot him in the thigh. Arborvitae's legs collapsed beneath him, and he tumbled over, rolling on the floor.

The three other soldiers remained wide-eyed with shock and held their positions as Arborvitae cried out, writhing in pain.

Jasper slowly got to his feet and retrieved a rifle from the corner. Vertiline watched him pull the cock back and check something. Then he trained the weapon awkwardly on the corporal.

Vertiline got up and moved away from the settee, straightening her clothes and covering her breasts. She never imagined Jasper and Merrill would see her unclothed. She should be mortified, but somehow felt no shame.

Mary had moved away from Limp Plug Tail. Carolee remained bound, on her side on the floor, a bruise blossoming on her right temple.

"Where's your father?" Merrill asked.

"Upstairs," Vertiline said. "He hasn't been well, but I'll go get him."

"No, miss. Just move back into the corner for now."

Vertiline did as he said.

"The fighting is over in these parts," the corporal said. "We hold the city."

"Either you men are lost," Merrill said, a grave look on his weathered face, "or you are deserters. Your army is a hundred miles east of here by now."

"You won't get away with this." The corporal was clearly feeling small and threatened. "We've taken all of Georgia."

"They were in too much of a hurry to set up camp here," Merrill said. "There's no one left to help you out. You men are alone with me and Jasper and these fine women."

"What are you going to do?"

Vertiline found the look of fear on the corporal's face satisfying.

"You can get up and leave or I can shoot you right where you sit. I'd prefer not to have to clean up the mess."

The corporal, Limp Plug Tail, and Gragston all stood slowly, their hands held out away from their sides.

"You'll be leaving your arms and supplies with us."

"We ain't got nothing," Limp Plug Tail said. "We're just hungry. Haven't eaten in days."

"Strange way to sate your appetite," Merrill said. "Jasper, move farther back so you can aim that damn thing."

Jasper limped to the other side of the room.

Merrill gestured toward the door as he moved away from the threshold. "Collect your brother, and get out," he said.

"Gragston, Lebleu, pack young Ward out of here," the corporal commanded. The two privates put their shoulders under the wounded man's arms and helped him hop out the door and down the hall to the entrance to the house. The corporal followed, Merrill keeping pace with him ten feet behind. The black man stopped near the entrance. He seemed to watch the soldiers leave the house and moved off down the street.

"If you come back here," he yelled, "I will make no further effort to preserve your lives."

Vertiline teetered for a moment, the world going dim around her. She stumbled back to the settee and collapsed. The tension of the last hour had taken everything out of her. Stuporous, she sat and watched the activity in the room.

Jasper leaned against the wall and slid heavily to the floor, his mouth still bleeding, his right eye swollen shut. Merrill came back into the parlor and cut Carolee out of her bonds. Mary walked to her twin and sat on the floor hugging her.

Merrill turned to Jasper. "I saw you leave the cave, and something about the way you looked over your shoulder told me you were up to no good," he said. "I'm glad I followed."

He walked over and kicked Jasper savagely in the thigh and the younger man bellowed his pain.

"Get up and get out, *now!*" Merrill shouted.

"I was hungry," Jasper said pitifully, his words garbled by the damage to his mouth, "and the soldiers said they'd take me in and there would be plenty for everyone, but I had to show good faith first by offering up some supplies."

"Out!" Merrill cried. He trained the pistol on Jasper's face.

Broken and bruised, the younger man pulled himself slowly, agonizingly to his feet.

Vertiline wanted to stop him, but she knew Merrill—he would not tolerate Jasper's betrayal. The younger slave took slow, heavy footsteps across the floor as he passed out of the house into the gathering dusk.

Vertiline could barely keep her eyes open. As Merrill mounted the stairs, she heard herself say, "Father," but she couldn't feel her voice anywhere; not in her mouth, throat, or lungs.

Her sisters were curled up on the floor. Exhausted, eyelids heavy, Vertiline allowed her eyes to close briefly...

...and then Mary was crying in the hall, at the foot of the stairs outside the parlor. "Where are you taking him?"

Vertiline rose and moved to see what was happening.

The twins stood talking in the hall with Merrill. He held Mr. Mortlow wrapped in a quilt and bent down to rest on one knee. The blanket covered all but Mr. Mortlow's pale, waxy face. Vertiline watched Carolee touch her father's grim, hollow cheek, then draw back quickly.

"He's gone," Merrill said.

"No," Vertiline whispered. She looked at Merrill. He *wanted* her father gone. He always wanted her father's authority.

"Yes, miss. He's been gone for a while."

Vertiline knew he spoke the truth, had known it in her heart for several days.

"He won't suffer anymore," Merrill said.

She reached out to touch her father, but then pulled her hand back. If she touched him, somehow that was saying goodbye, and she couldn't face that. She had no strength and needed sleep. Later would come proper mourning.

The twins wept. Mary stumbled away, exhausted, headed back to the parlor. After a moment, Carolee followed.

"I'm going to take him out and prepare a box for him," Merrill said. "Then I'm going to find us food. For now, sleep." He lifted his burden and passed out of the house.

Vertiline returned to the settee.

She awoke to discover that she had been covered with quilts from the hiding place. So had her sisters. Again, they slept, curled together on the floor. Vertiline's shoes had been put on her feet.

Night had fallen, but the moon was bright. She struggled up the stairs to find her father, but he wasn't in his study. Then she remembered he had passed away, that Merrill said he'd make a box in which to bury him.

She walked back downstairs and out the front door. The frigid night surrounded her, but she didn't feel cold. A warm smell came from the southeast side of the house and she moved in that direction, walking awkwardly up the drive to the carriage house. Orange light shone from the high windows of the structure. The odor was stronger.

The smell of cooking meat!

She opened the double doors. Merrill was leaning over a table at the cluttered back end of the carriage house. Startled by her arrival, he swung around suddenly, a cup of something in his left hand sloshing liquid onto the floor. His right hand moved to the pistol tucked under his belt, but relaxed when he seemed to recognize her.

"What did you find to eat?" Vertiline asked, dizzied by the wonderful odor.

Merrill set the cup down. "I found a horse dead in the street a short distance from here," he said. "I'm boiling some of the meat now. Go back in the house and wait for me there, and I'll bring it for you and your sisters when it's done, very soon."

Merrill had fired up the old cooking stove that had been put in the carriage house to provide warmth when needed. A large pot sat on the metal heating surface, steam and the delicious aroma rising from its interior in plumes. She didn't want to leave that incredible smell.

"What of Father?"

The question seemed to shock Merrill. She'd never seen him anything other than confident. "I built him a box," he said, pointing across the room. "Tomorrow, we'll place him in the garden."

Vertiline spared a glance at the makeshift coffin as she moved toward Merrill, but her goal was to get closer to the pot of savory warmth.

As she moved, she saw the dark blood smeared on the work table behind Merrill.

"The horse meat made a mess," he said. "You don't want to come over here, Miss Mortlow."

A long strip of pink skin with sparse, tiny hairs, like those on a man's leg, lay on the table, illuminated in the moonlight coming from the window and the light of a lamp. She'd never seen a horse with a hide like that.

Merrill saw her looking at the skin and seemed to move to his left to hide it behind him.

"Why are you…?" she began. Her voice trailed off as because the proper question was, *What are you hiding?*

Something was terribly wrong. Nevertheless, curiosity and hunger kept her moving.

Merrill sagged a little, took a breath and looked her in the eye. "I didn't want to do this, but needs must," he said. "If you girls don't eat, you'll soon die." His voice sounded warm and caring, but he looked savage with the dark blood on his hands and exposed forearms. "The last thing your father has to offer you—"

A few more steps and she would stand beside him.

And, suddenly, she knew with a certainty that the delicious aroma rising from the pot was her father.

Vertiline wanted to turn and run, but as if in a dream, she didn't have complete control over herself. She still moved forward through the cluttered area to get to the food. The best she could do was to stop her legs. They collapsed beneath her and she fell toward Merrill. If he hadn't caught her, she would have struck her head on the corner of the table.

Merrill lifted and cradled her in his arms. She struggled, but in her weakened condition, he easily overcame her efforts without harm. Vertiline opened her mouth to speak, but he spoke first.

"I couldn't save him this time. The soldiers didn't harm him, he perished from lack of food."

Still cradling her, he lowered himself and sat on the floor.

"Your father was a brave man. We fought in in the Texas War of Independence. I know he didn't tell you about it. My master, a man by the name of Parsons, took me to war with him. Parsons was killed and I would have been as well, but for your father's heroism. He saved my life, and it's a good thing, because I had the chance to save his life before the fighting ended. After the war, I asked him to buy me from the Parsons family, and I've been with him since."

The story was something out of a dream. How could it be true? Still, what he said did make sense out of her father's unusual bond with Merrill.

"Your father died a man of courage while protecting those he loved. The power of that still lives in his flesh, along with his wisdom and experience."

"No…no…" Vertiline protested weakly. She pushed and pulled at his powerful arms, but she had no strength.

"My mother was Carib Indian from the West Indies. The tradition in my family is to take inside our bodies a little of the flesh of our men and women, those of strength and character who have gone before us. If I'm a strong and good man, it's because my father and his father were good, and live inside me now. If I'm kind and humble, it's because I carry in my flesh those traits of my mother and her mother. They live still, just as your father will when you and your sisters take him inside." He made a slow pantomime of eating.

Vertiline's hunger became stronger.

Merrill reached up and retrieved his cup of tea. "Drink," he said.

Vertiline took the cup and raised it to her lips. Not tea at all, the liquid smelled like broth. As her mouth watered, she knew the brew was made from her father. She could not stop her hands and lips, mouth and throat. The warmth poured into her and spread life through her limbs, her head, eyes, ears, nose, and mouth. She dropped the empty cup. "More," she cried hoarsely, and pushed against his arms to get free.

Merrill held her until she became calm. "Not yet. You must go and prepare the kitchen."

He released her.

Vertiline stood slowly and turned to look at the steaming pot. "How long?" she asked.

As he stood, he pulled his watch from his tattered vest, held it in the moonlight, and looked at its face. "Half an hour. We'll sit down and eat properly, all four of us. Now go. Don't tell your sisters."

Vertiline stood a moment, reflecting. Merrill fed her the flesh of her father! She had committed a horrible crime that placed her outside of all of human society. If anyone found out, she'd be hounded out of any community she tried to join for the rest of her life.

He would make her sisters commit the crime without their knowledge. They would become outcasts if anyone found out.

Merrill also drank the broth! He was a cannibal, a savage. He'd always been, but had tricked her father into trusting him.

Was that his plan all along? Did he, in truth, kill their father as part of that plan?

Merrill watched her with a reassuring steadiness, his face calm. Despite her resentment toward him, she knew his commitment to her family had always been absolute. She'd never known him to lie. He wasn't a devious man.

"It's up to you, miss," Merrill said. "I can keep looking, but time's getting short for all of us."

No, he didn't kill her father. Vertiline knew in her heart that her father was dead. Mr. Mortlow told her he would die, and left her in charge of her sisters. The decision was indeed hers now, not Merrill's. She must decide whether to feed her sisters the only food available.

Vertiline took another look at the steaming pot.

No one would ever know, and she would keep the truth from the twins. Mary and Carolee would live.

Vertiline turned and slowly made her way back to the house. As she passed through the darkness and the moonlight, she was horrified...and invigorated.

While the twins slept, curled together on the parlor floor, Vertiline went to the kitchen and cleaned up much of the mess made by the various intruders. When the table was clean, she located plates, cups, and silverware, and began to set the table. After the damage done by the looters, many cups were broken, but quite a few suffered only chips or missing handles. The roughest of silverware was all that remained, those the slaves had been allowed to use. She found two unbroken plates, most of another one missing a chunk, and another broken cleanly into two parts. Vertiline placed the pieces together on the table so they appeared to be a whole plate. She found clean napkins in the back of a drawer and added them to the place-settings.

Vertiline wished she had more to do so she didn't have to think about what was coming. Finished with preparations in the kitchen, she retreated into the darkness at the top of the stairs to keep watch. Draped with two quilts and hugging the banister newel at the top of the stairs, Vertiline kept her eyes on the front entrance to the house. She looked between the balusters as if through the bars of a cell. The door still lay shattered on the front stoop. A brief shower had occurred while she was in the kitchen. The moisture had frozen, leaving a clear, shiny coating on the door and everything else outside.

She hoped the aroma of cooking in the carriage house would not draw the attention of strangers. The structure was well off the road out front, but anyone who wandered down Spring Street might become aware of the smell. Hopefully, the slick, frozen world outside kept anyone within the vicinity indoors.

As if Vertiline could make it so by will alone, she imagined the house gave an impression that it was totally abandoned and contained nothing of value. She imagined an invisible barrier in the doorway to keep her family safe. She tried to believe with conviction that no more Union soldiers or freed slaves would gain entrance to her home, and that she'd already seen the worst of the war.

When Merrill appeared in the doorway, the horror of anticipating the meal to come tumbled down on her, but hunger pushed the dread aside, and she rose to greet him. He carried the steaming pot to the kitchen and placed it on the table.

After surveying her work with the place settings, he looked at her curiously and a bit sadly. Vertiline didn't know what to make of it, but he quickly turned back to the business at hand, lifting the lid of the pot and ladling out four cups of broth.

She must not think.

Vertiline lifted a cup, blew on the liquid to cool it and drank, trying to imagine the brew was merely tea. Delicious and rich, the drink brought warmth and a feeling of rejuvenation, but also shame.

Merrill skewered a small piece of meat, about a quarter of a pound in weight. He placed the morsel on an unbroken plate.

Looking at it, Vertiline's mouth watered, redoubling her shame. *It's only meat, much like what I've eaten all my life.*

Merrill cut the flesh into four small portions.

"I must find a place to allow the rest of this to cool where it will be hidden," Merrill said.

"Is that all we'll eat?" Vertiline asked. Hunger had won out over the shame. The table was set for a big meal—she wanted a large portion to sink her teeth into.

"We must start slowly or you and your sisters will become ill."

Though it took her a few moments, she decided she should trust him to know best. She nodded her head, feeling foolish about setting the table. She realized that when he'd said, "prepare the kitchen," he'd merely meant for her to clean it up.

"Perhaps taking it back to the carriage house would be best," Merrill said.

"A spring house!" Vertiline said, remembering her discovery. "I found one on the Shannons' property. It's hidden at the back of their garden."

"I'd forgotten about that. Yes, that would be good."

Vertiline took up a lamp and led him out the kitchen door and through the back garden.

"Where's Agnes?" she asked as they walked.

"My poor wife," he said, the words long and drawn out with sadness, his breath puffing out pale vapor into the cold air. "We were hiding at Fischer's Cave, but we had no food and had to leave. When the Union Army was moving through, we followed because we could scavenge their camps each time they moved on. There wasn't much to be found. We were part of a growing crowd of slaves with no home; hundreds, perhaps a thousand or more. Word came the troops dumped some wormy meal. There was a stampede to get to it. Agnes, along with several others, was trampled to death."

"I'm sorry," Vertiline said.

"She was a sweet woman."

They passed through the hole in the privet hedge. After lighting the lamp, they moved into the spring house. Merrill left the pot of broth and meat on a broad shelf high on the wall, and then they went back to the house.

"You returned to the cave before coming here?"

"Yes, miss. A creek runs out of the cave, with minnows, crawfish, and sala-manders, but there's nothing left there, at least for a while."

Merrill lifted two of the steaming cups from the kitchen table. "Carry these into the parlor, Miss Mortlow, and wake the twins. When they've drunk the broth, we must give them time to digest it."

Merrill lifted the plate with the meat. "Later, we'll serve this." He placed it in a cabinet on a shelf, out of sight.

Following their small meal, all three of the sisters complained of stomach aches through the night, but felt much better and invigorated the next morning.

At noon they sat down to another meal. They were each served approxi-mately a quarter of a pound of meat. Carolee and Mary both smiled. Pleased that the twins were at least momentarily happy, Vertiline's heavy heart had lifted some as well. Merrill ate silently, his expression unreadable and stoic. Vertiline's imagination finally gave in and allowed her to disregard the fact that the flesh was part of her father. The meat had a mild taste. If not for some toughness, she might have compared it to veal.

"Carolee has food on her chin," Mary said, pointing and laughing.

"It's stringy," Carolee said, opening her mouth to show the meat caught in her teeth.

Vertiline let it go—good manners could wait until they were healthy again.

"That horse must have been an old nag," Carolee continued, "tired from working the fields."

Vertiline easily laughed the words off. The twins seemed to feel well. They were going to survive. These events would become part of the past; if not forgotten, certainly remembered as a time in which they joyfully triumphed over adversity. The twins would grow up, get married, and have families. Life would become ordinary again. The future would be bright.

The moment before Carolee bit down on her next mouthful, her smile was so large, the frown that followed seemed comical. Mary laughed and pointed again, but Carolee wasn't playing. She opened her mouth and spit out the mouthful. The masticated meat hit her plate and out of the mess rolled a bright golden ball.

Merrill gripped the table, but immediately tried to relax.

Vertiline didn't understand what she was looking at. Perhaps, somehow, the yellow marble she'd found in the spring house and put in the pocket of her father's coat had found its way into the cooking pot.

No, Carolee's bite marks dented the surface of the ball—the thing was definitely gold.

Mary stared incredulous and smiling slightly, as if Carolee were playing a joke.

Carolee, her mouth and eyes held wide, stared in horror a moment longer. Then the truth seemed to dawn on her the same instant Vertiline saw the ball for what it was. Carolee's mouth sagged into a grimace, and she pushed back from the table so violently, her chair toppled over backwards, taking her with it. She got up and ran screaming from the kitchen, through the dining room and hall, and out the front door of the house.

Merrill and Vertiline went after her. Carolee ran northwest on Spring Street and then turned up a drive and ran behind a house. Merrill gained on her, but she crawled through bushes and into the property beyond. He tried to leap over the bushes, crashed into them, rolled to the other side, and ran the direction Carolee had taken.

Vertiline backtracked and went around, gaining access to the property through the garden next door.

"Over here," Merrill called, and she caught up with him as he crouched, pulling the broken lattice away from the base of a porch. "She's in there."

He crawled in and disappeared into the shadows. "Come along, Miss Carolee," he said. "Come to Merrill. Everything's going to be all right."

Vertiline heard a scuffle and then Merrill bellowed. "She bit me!"

Then he was backing out, pulling Carolee along by the ankle. When he got his feet under himself, he hauled her up into the air, holding her upside-down at arm's length. Growling and screaming, Carolee thrashed and swung and lunged with her teeth. She got a grip on Merrill's thigh and bit down. He cried out in pain, but didn't let go. "She's like an animal," he shouted.

Shocked, Vertiline hardly recognized the feral beast as her sister.

"Do something!" Merrill cried.

Vertiline stepped up and wrapped her hands around Carolee's neck, pulling her away from his leg. Blood welled up from the wound and soaked his trousers.

Maintaining her grip with one hand, Vertiline picked up a stout stick with the other. The next time Carolee opened her mouth to scream, Vertiline put the wood between her sister's teeth and held onto the ends from behind her. Merrill lowered Carolee quickly and flipped her onto her back. Vertiline held onto the stick and Merrill pinned Carolee's limbs to the ground. The girl bucked against them until exhausted and lay panting around the stick.

"We had to eat it or we would have died," Vertiline said. "You must understand, Carolee. It's done. You're alive and so are the rest of us. Father would have wanted us to live, to make that choice. Because he loved you, no sacrifice was too great for him to make for you."

Carolee glared at Vertiline, then shifted her horrible stare to Merrill. Finally Carolee looked up at the blue sky. The fight was gone from her. The older sister could feel the younger one relaxing. Slowly, Vertiline let go and pulled the stick from Carolee's mouth. Vertiline brushed debris that had come from under the porch, cobwebs and insect chitin, out of her little sister's hair.

Merrill let go, and Vertiline helped Carolee stand.

"Come with me," Vertiline said. "I won't hurt you. We'll go home and forget all about what happened today. You don't have to remember if you don't want to. It could be a big joke or maybe it's just not what you thought it was."

Her voice had a calming effect. Carolee became compliant, and they made their way home.

Mary was still seated at the table in the kitchen, her eyes locked on the golden bullet, her hands together in prayer, her mouth working silently.

Merrill scooped up the ball and slipped it into his pocket.

⚜

The twins fell asleep mid-afternoon on a pile of quilts on the parlor floor, and did not awaken until the next day.

Vertiline sat listening to their breathing, trying to keep her eyes on them while Merrill sewed up the hole Carolee put in his leg and the one in his trousers. He sat in her father's favorite chair and got blood on the upholstery, but it didn't matter. When he was done, he finally spoke to Vertiline about the gold bullet.

"I'm so sorry, miss. I'd forgotten all about the bullet or I would never have chosen...."

He stopped and hung his head.

151

"Everyone knew he'd fought the duel with that man from Atlanta," Merrill said. "He found a reason for me not to attend him on that day because he knew I'd never let him go through with it. I didn't see what was loaded into those pistols, so I never truly believed."

Merrill hung his head for a moment, then looked at Vertiline. "Mr. Mortlow told me he was a mediocre lawyer, but that doing away with Clarence Perforce Tate had brought him notoriety and respect. He said he might not have risen to such high office if it hadn't been for his luck in dispatching the man. But *nobody* believed he truly had a solid gold bullet lodged in his thigh."

Still watching her sisters, Vertiline felt her features take on a grim smile as a sadly humorous thought occurred to her. "When he told us that story, he always said, 'If we ever run on hard times, I will cut it out and we'll be rich again.'"

She turned to face Merrill and looked him in the eye. He was not smiling.

"You did your best for us," she said. "You're a free man now. You take that bullet and make a start for yourself. I never want to see it again."

❧

"Are you all right, Miss Mortlow?" Merrill asked.

The guard stepped over to take a look at her. Vertiline glanced up at him and nodded, and he stepped back to the door.

Vertiline's heartbeat slowed and the distress at seeing Merrill diminished. She produced a weak smile and he returned it.

"I've grown old and delicate, that's all," she said.

"Delicate, perhaps," he said, "as a fine woman should be, but old? I have reached my ninety-fifth year."

He had lived to a fine old age. Vertiline allowed warm feelings for Merrill to push back against the fear of remembrance. Since the end of the War, memories of him had always brought with them the terrors of that time. More care might have been made in his decisions, but he truly meant the best in what he'd done for her family. They had all survived the war and lived their lives. He'd made that possible.

"In the newspaper, I read about your troubles, those of you and your sisters."

Vertiline looked away. He might think poorly of them after what he'd read.

"There's no need to say anything about it, miss."

Vertiline was grateful, but then nothing occurred to her to help further the conversation.

He bowed his head. "I'm sorry to hear of the loss of your sister."

Vertiline couldn't allow herself to think about Mary yet.

"I truly came to see if you have need. A delicate matter, I know, but when they find you innocent and you're released, do you and Mrs. Marshall have—" he was clearly uncomfortable speaking about such things to a white woman. "—a proper home and the funds to live as you need to? I heard the house in East Orange burned, and I'm concerned that you will have little to return to."

"I truly don't know what we'll do, but decisions will have to wait until this

152

terrible business is over."

Merrill was silent for a moment, then seemed to gather himself. "After the War, I invested your gift in a small business in Pittsburg, Pennsylvania, selling sausages on the street. When I earned enough, I rented a small store front downtown and ran a tavern, The Old Forge, for many years. I saved my money, and five years ago opened a small hotel with a restaurant. Do you remember Ducy's cooking?"

Vertiline hadn't thought of her old governess in a long time. She hadn't had the likes of Ducy's cooking since she was a child. Smiling, she thought of the old woman's French toast. Her cooking had been a large part of the magic of the garden parties Vertiline remembered so fondly from her early childhood.

"I have her recipes." Merrill said. "Her soups, roasts, and desserts are our customers' favorites."

The thought brought a smile to Vertiline's face. "I'm glad you've done well. Ducy would have liked that her recipes survived her."

They sat and regarded one another comfortably for a moment.

"The hotel's name is Sweet Agnes, after my wife," Merrill said with a slight smile. "You remember her."

Vertiline nodded.

"We serve white patrons, and some don't take kindly to the idea that a black man owns the hotel. The people of Pennsylvania aren't bad sorts, but they have fears just like everyone."

She thought of the anger she'd seen in the eyes of the twelve men on the jury in her trial, and knew that much of it was a reflection of how she felt about herself. Although hard to admit, shame for having brought ruin to her family, and nothing more, had made looking squarely at people during the trial so difficult. To look at them was to see her own disapproval staring back.

Merrill was right; the people of the North were much like those of the South or anywhere else. They were petty and small, but also capable of thoughtful decisions and noble sacrifices when needed.

"If graced by the presence of refined ladies, such as yourself and your sister, the front desk of the hotel would be complete. It could only do my business good. I would offer you room and board, and you could take on as many or as few duties as you'd like."

He wants a white presence at the front desk. Still, I'm but one of many from whom he could choose. Perhaps he still feels he owes something to Father.

"A generous offer for a suspected criminal," Vertiline said with a grim smile.

"I would not have had the opportunities I've had in life, if not for your gift. It's only fitting that I help you in your time of need."

Vertiline could hardly speak as she considered his kind words. Had she performed an unselfish act at least once in her life, something worthy of reward? Somehow, she could not see it, but felt grateful to hear him speak of it nonetheless.

Finally Vertiline pulled herself together. "Thank you, but—" Unexpected tears welled up in her eyes. "—the state believes in its case against me, and Carolee has been…indisposed of late."

Merrill showed no signs of distress upon seeing her emotion. "Your father left you with a difficult task. Your sisters were—" Again, he looked uncomfortable. "—high-spirited."

Vertiline couldn't help but chuckle as the tears fell from her eyes.

He smiled knowingly. "I'm sure you did your best, and your father would be proud of you."

Vertiline wondered if that were true.

Merrill stood and offered her a slip of paper. "My calling card," he said. "You'll find me at that address. Please come to me if you have need, you and your sister."

"Thank you again." She reached to shake his hand as she had seen her father do. His grasp was warm and comforting.

The guard let Merrill out, and then led Vertiline back to her cell.

Chapter 18
Vertiline—Acceptance

Mr. Hitchens met with Vertiline in her jail cell early Thursday morning. "Against the new charge, we can try an insanity defense," he said.

The attorney withered under the power of her gaze. Vertiline could never permit others to see her as insane. Still, she thought about it, not to consider the possibility that she was mad, but seriously wondering about herself, her role in the dreadful events of the past few decades. Ever since Merrill's visit, she'd thought about whether her father would be proud of her.

"If you're cleared on the original charges," Mr. Hitchens said, "but convicted of obstruction of justice in the disappearance of your niece's son, you would not be given a sentence longer than five years. You might win an acquittal—their case against you regarding the missing infant is weak."

He truly seemed to care about what happened to her, and Vertiline realized in that moment that he always had.

"Yes, but if I don't accept their offer and my sister becomes well again, she will be tried for the original charges, and for aiding and abetting in John's disappearance. She was there when he was lost. They have a better case against her."

"That's correct," Mr. Hitchens said. He took up his leather case. "Let me know what you decide about the prosecution's offer by four-thirty this afternoon."

"I will."

Mr. Hitchens left Vertiline to her thoughts.

Her father had put the twins in her hands, not merely to protect them, but to guide them, to teach them how to get along in the world as they found it— the way the world was, not the way they thought it should be.

The War Between the States had officially ended almost fifty years earlier, but Vertiline had continued the war secretly, while choosing to believe that was exactly what the Federal government did. She allowed the sort of extreme measures necessary for survival during the war to continue in peacetime. Living among the enemy, as she'd seen it, Vertiline had chosen again and again to excuse the family's crimes as the cost of survival. Presently, the choices seemed those of a lunatic.

The fateful meal Vertiline fed her sisters so long ago had taken them all beyond the pale. Lost in uncharted wilderness, the twins needed their big sister to guide them back to the embrace of human society, but Vertiline had failed to find the way. With her conspiracies against the insurance companies, the disastrous marriage she'd forced on Carolee, and offenses against Winifred concerning the will, Vertiline had not been a good example. The responsibility for the twins' crimes belonged to her.

The question remained: Would Carolee still be a danger if she became well and was released?

At the age of fifty-nine, she was too old to cause much trouble, and no doubt several years would pass before she recovered, if she ever did.

The right thing was to accept the prosecution's offer and take the punishment for Carolee as she had done when Agnes fell and broke her arm almost fifty years ago. She remembered her father's face on that day, shining down on her like the warm sun in a perfect, cloudless sky.

If Carolee ever earned her freedom, Vertiline would make sure she went to Merrill. He would take care of her.

With the decision made, a calm settled over her, and she relaxed for the first time in a long while.

Vertiline's throat had become so tight and painful over the last month, she could hardly eat. The meals at the prison weren't very appetizing, but she missed them when she could no longer tolerate solid food. Even liquids had become difficult to swallow. The persistent empty feeling in her stomach, and the weakness she experience from lack of nourishment took her back to cruel memories of the War. When the doctor in the prison infirmary told her she had cancer and would not live much longer, she'd felt some relief. She'd done all she could do in life, and saw herself as old and useless. Her arthritis made each day an arduous undertaking. She was ready for a long rest.

Five days earlier, Vertiline had been given a bed in the infirmary, and the doctor said she'd only live for a few more days.

Carolee came for a visit. She sat in a chair a trustee orderly had placed beside Vertiline's bed. The younger sister's skirt and bodice were a forest green, a color that spoke of life, and she looked healthy and happy.

Vertiline tried to have a conversation with her, but talking was painful. She settled for listening and holding her sister's hand.

"Of course it's nice to be out and a part of the world again," Carolee said, "but my thoughts have been with you."

Vertiline squeezed her hand, tried to speak again, and failed.

"Don't try to talk," her sister said. Carolee seemed restless as she stood to look through the narrow window to the right of the bed. Vertiline knew that her sister looked toward the prison yard below, that she saw the walls topped with barbed wire, the women in uniform gray shift dresses standing in clusters or walking along the paths, many of them smoking. Of course Carolee was restless—she'd spent her share of time in a prison of sorts and no doubt fought off a desire to flee Vertiline's place of confinement.

"To be ill while away from family is always a hardship," Carolee said. "I want to stay here with you until the end, but they'll only allow me to be here for a short time."

Seeing her sister, however short the visit, pleased Vertiline, but she wished they could spend the time together in private. The infirmary was a long, narrow white room with a vaulted ceiling. Beds were situated against the exterior wall every ten feet with no partitions between them. Coughing, moaning, and the murmur of conversation were periodic distractions. The occupant of the bed to Vertiline's left made no effort to conceal her interest in Carolee's words. Vertiline could hardly blame the prisoner—existence in the infirmary was dreadfully dull.

"I enjoy Pittsburg more than I did Brooklyn. The people are friendlier and there aren't so many different kinds of folks."

Vertiline wondered if her sister had been afraid of some of the people in Brooklyn. She knew that Carolee, too, was a "different kind" of person.

Almost a year ago, shortly after Vertiline was transferred to prison, alienists at the sanatorium declared Carolee cured, and she was released. Vertiline made certain that Carolee received instructions about how to find Merrill. As planned, he took her in and everything seemed to go well.

Carolee sat back down and took up Vertiline's hand. "There's news I'm reluctant to tell you," she said, bowing her head, "but perhaps knowing, you will more easily find him on the other side."

Vertiline had never heard Carolee refer to "the other side" or make any other spiritual reference for that matter. Something had changed.

"Merrill has passed away," her sister said.

Alarmed, Vertiline had to remind herself that Merrill had been quite elderly. Her thoughts turned to concern for her sister, and what the occurrence might mean for Carolee's future. The older sister wanted to ask how the man had died, but even if she could, she wasn't sure she'd want to hear the answer. What if Carolee said he'd taken a fatal fall?

No, I mustn't think that! I won't think it!

"Please don't worry about my welfare," Carolee said. "He left me the hotel."

Vertiline squeezed her eyes shut and banished the image in her head of Merrill lying dead at the foot of a staircase.

He was ninety-six years old. Surely he died naturally.

Vertiline opened her eyes and did her best to give Carolee a genuine smile.

About the Author

Alan M. Clark, fine arts painter, illustrator, and author hails from Tennessee, where he grew up in a house full of human bones and old medical books. At present, he lives in Eugene, Oregon with his wife, Melody. In his 33 year freelance career, he has created illustrations for hundreds of books, including works of fiction of various genres, nonfiction, textbooks, young adult fiction, and children's books. He is the author of seventeen books, including eleven novels, a lavishly illustrated novella, four collections of fiction, and a nonfiction full-color book of his artwork. The World Fantasy Award and four Chesley Awards are among the honors he's received for his work. Mr. Clark's company, IFD Publishing, has released forty-four books, including hardcovers, paperbacks, ebooks, and audio books. IFD Publishing's authors include F. Paul Wilson, Elizabeth Engstrom, and Jeremy Robert Johnson. www.alanmclark.com

Connect with the Author Online.
You can email the author or find out more about him through the following websites:
http://www.ifdpublishing.com
http://www.smashwords.com/profile/view/IFDPublishing

IFD Publishing Paperbacks

Novels:
Death is a Star, by Christina Lay
Baggage Check, by Elizabeth Engstrom
Bull's Labyrinth, by Eric Witchey
The Surgeon's Mate: A Dismemoir, by Alan M. Clark
Siren Promised, by Jeremy Robert Johnson and Alan M. Clark
Say Anything but Your Prayers, by Alan M. Clark
Candyland, by Elizabeth Engstrom
Apologies to the Cat's Meat Man, by Alan M. Clark

Collections:
Professor Witchey's Miracle Mood Cure, by Eric Witchey

Nonfiction:
How to Write a Sizzling Sex Scene, by Elizabeth Engstrom

IFD Publishing EBooks

(You can find the following titles at most distribution points for all ereading platforms.)

Novels:
Bull's Labyrinth, by Eric Witchey
The Surgeon's Mate: A Dismemoir, by Alan M. Clark
York's Moon, by Elizabeth Engstrom
Beyond the Serpent's Heart, by Eric Witchey
Lizzie Borden, by Elizabeth Engstrom
A Parliament of Crows, by Alan M. Clark
Lizard Wine, by Elizabeth Engstrom
Northwoods Chronicles: A Novel in Short Stories, by Elizabeth Engstrom
Siren Promised, by Alan M. Clark and Jeremy Robert Johnson
To Kill a Common Loon, by Mitch Luckett
The Man in the Loon, by Mitch Luckett
Jack the Ripper Victim Series: Of Thimble and Threat by Alan M. Clark
Jack the Ripper Victim Series: The Double Event (includes two novels from the series: *Of Thimble and Threat* and *Say Anything But Your Prayers*) by Alan M. Clark
Candyland, by Elizabeth Engstrom
The Blood of Father Time: Book 1, The New Cut, by Alan M. Clark, Stephen C. Merritt & Lorelei Shannon
The Blood of Father Time: Book 2, The Mystic Clan's Grand Plot, by Alan M. Clark, Stephen C. Merritt & Lorelei Shannon

How I Met My Alien Bitch Lover: Book 1 from the Sunny World Inquisition Daily Letter Archives, by Eric Witchey
Baggage Check, by Elizabeth Engstrom
Death is a Star, by Christina Lay
D. D. Murphry, Secret Policeman, by Alan M. Clark and Elizabeth Massie
Black Leather, by Elizabeth Engstrom

Novelettes:
The Tao of Flynn, by Eric Witchey
To Build a Boat, Listen to Trees, by Eric Witchey

Children's Illustrated:
The Christmas Thingy, by F. Paul Wilson. Illustrated by Alan M. Clark

Collections:
Suspicions, by Elizabeth Engstrom
Professor Witchey's Miracle Mood Cure, by Eric Witchey

Short Fiction:
"Brittle Bones and Old Rope," by Alan M. Clark
"Crosley," by Elizabeth Engstrom
"The Apple Sniper," by Eric Witchey

Nonfiction:
How to Write a Sizzling Sex Scene by Elizabeth Engstrom

IFD Publishing Audio Books

Novels:
The Door That Faced West by Alan M. Clark, read by Charles Hinckley
Jack the Ripper Victim Series: Of Thimble and Threat by Alan M. Clark, read by Alicia Rose
Jack the Ripper Victim Series: Say Anything But Your Prayers by Alan M. Clark, read by Alicia Rose
Jack the Ripper Victim Series: The Double Event by Alan M. Clark, read by Alicia Rose (includes two novels from the series: *Of Thimble and Threat* and *Say Anything But Your Prayers*)
A Parliament of Crows by Alan M. Clark, read by Laura Jennings
A Brutal Chill in August by Alan M. Clark, read by Alicia Rose
The Surgeon's Mate: A Dismemoir by Alan M. Clark, read by Alan M. Clark
Apologies to the Cat's Meat Man by Alan M. Clark, read by Alicia Rose